MW01145393

Sleep!

Thank you

[signature]

Night mares of a Mad man

John W. Smith

Nightmares of a Madman

This book is manufactured in the United States. This is a work of fiction; Names, characters, places, and incidents are the product of the author's imagination, or are used fictitiously. Any resemblance to actual persons, living or dead, is entirely coincidental.

Copyright © 2013 John Smith
All rights reserved.

No parts of this book may be reproduced in any form or by any electronic or mechanical means including photocopying, recording, or by information retrieval and retrieval systems, without permission in writing from the publisher, except by a reviewer, who may quote brief passages in a review.

All rights reserved.
Published in the United States by Well Read Press

ISBN 978-0-9891810-0-6
Soft Cover
E-Book 978-0-9891810-1-3

Library of Congress Number 2013946112

FIRST EDITION

Publisher: Well Read Press
PO Box 12545 State Route 143 Suite C #128
Highland, ILL 62249

John W. Smith
Nightmares of a Madman
For bulk orders contact wellreadpress@gmail.com
Contact the author:
writerphotographer1946@gmail.com
Author Website: www.JohnWSmithAuthor.com

Advanced Praise for

Nightmares of a Madman

John Smith writes with fingernails dipped in blood. The unexpected is expected with twists and turns that lead the reader to crypts of shivers and sleepless nights ... This book should be read at night, behind locked doors, with only a reading light focused on the pages. A strong drink may dull the senses, delaying the full anguish of the mind until the following sleepless night ...

—Charles "Chuck" Schwend, author of
Dragon Dreams, Words to Read, and *Gulag #7*

One remembers life is for living and best remembered in the small gifts received, sometimes small revenges in retribution of the scars earned in life. John Smith's gift to us is that he reminds us all...'wait your turn, your chance is coming to make things right.'

—Jaime Cancio, photographer

John Smith takes you on a twisted ride through the macabre. Each tale is a glimpse into the dark corners of a madman's mind.

—Kat Perry, author of *The Calm*

Dedication

I want to thank everyone who helped me with this book. The *Highland League of Writers* and the *Ocular Voices* writing groups. Without these two groups, I would never have written the stories. They were the first to listen and to offer ideas, suggestions, and encouragement.

Thanks to Sandy Maue, Jaime 'The Rebel' Cancio, Linda Bemis, and Russell Glenn who helped edit all the stories.

Special Thanks to Kasey Kemper who kept my computer functional.

Thanks to Peggy and Larry DeKay who became my guides, mentors, and assisted in making this book a reality.

To my Mom, who believed I could write a book with a faith that never wavered.

Contents

In the *Evil World* ...

There are no Rules

"William Stanley." The voice boomed through the speakers. The judge stared directly at William, his face glaring through the six-foot image on the video screen. The hard set of his jaw made the judge more intimidating—fierce.

"You have been found guilty of crimes against society. It is time for your sentencing." His voice boomed from the speakers hidden in the walls.

"Wait, you can't do that," William answered, his voice cracking. "There's been no trial! What have I done?"

The stony image of the Judge glistened in silent condemnation as he moved the paper from one side of the bench. Hard-faced, he said nothing.

"The facts have been reviewed, Mr. Stanley, you are guilty of not maintaining the *status quo*. You have mastered your studies, volunteer work, and student employment. You failed to listen to your teachers and superiors. You have chosen to excel. You have refused to be average—insisting on surpassing your peers, and lowering their self-esteem. William Nelson Whitney, you are condemned; your life forfeit. May God have mercy on your soul."

William thought he saw the slightest grin breaking on the edges of the Judges thin lips.

"This is insane, I'll appeal," the sweat beaded on his forehead, his breath coming in quick puffs.

He knew his life depended on his ability to reverse the execution decision. There was no one to come to his aid or overturn his conviction.

The judge's hand paused above the shutdown button. The camera focused on a shot of William's face. "Sir, there is no appeal. You have failed. You continued to excel. Even now, you question authority. For the record, your reports of failure were provided by written statements of your peers, superiors, and through various historical reviews." He rested his hand on a thick folder in front of the camera.

"Happy birthday, today you are an adult; your sentence is to be carried out immediately. Your family will be notified." The judge's hand hovered over the button. The last thing William saw was the tip of a long, boney finger, capped by a grimy, nicotine stained nail. The screen went black.

Four large muscular men, with no necks and zero body fat surrounded William. "Do we need to chain you or will you walk with us?" one of them asked.

"I'll walk," whispered William. He turned, his body deflated like a spent helium balloon, he walked between the four men.

William entered a world of concrete and cinderblock. Screened florescent lights gave everything an acid green haze. If this was his new life, William hoped it would end soon.

They reached the end of the hall. William was steered to the left by the strong arms of his captors, and shoved into a small room.

"Strip and shower, you have five minutes."

His clothing falling at his feet. The door closed as water poured from the ceiling. There was no room to turn around or bend, so he stood, allowing the water to flow over his body.

Turning the soap in his hands, he worked up a good lather. A strong, antiseptic order invaded his nostrils. His skin burned as the lather rested on his arms.

A door opened in front of him revealing one of the four guards. Naked and wet, William did as he was told, and stepped onto the ramp. It began to move forward. Hot air blew from all directions, drying him. At the end of the ramp, one of the guards handed him a paper gown.

"All this seems to be a bit much for someone you are going to execute," William said. The guard pointed to a long hallway that seemed to lead nowhere. Still under escort, the five walked down the hall.

William fell into step with his escorts for about one hundred yards when they came to a stop in front of a gray metal door.

One of the guards knocked three times and the door opened. William couldn't see over the two escorts in front of him, but he could smell something— something horrifying ... formaldehyde.

His legs weakened as he was assaulted by the odor. This was the smell of a medical lab or a death chamber. The rear guards gave William a gentle push as they entered the room.

William kept his eyes and head forward. Taking short breaths, he knew he was about to be put to death.

"Welcome, Mr. Stanley," A voice echoed throughout the room. "Welcome to your new home."

The two front guards stepped aside. William saw a chair made of metal framework and some kind of cloth webbing that created what could have been a comfortable recliner, had it been covered with padding.

The guards guided William to the chair, holding him by his elbows. His mouth was slack. He had been prepared to die, but torture was something else. His body seemed to cave in on itself.

All for their sick entertainment, he thought to himself. *I don't know any state secrets*. He had wanted to be noticed—to move up in the political realms and have a better life. He had the drive and ambition to be one of those in charge of the country. He knew he did.

He walked to the chair and sank into the seat. He said nothing as the guards began to strap his body to the device. Head first, followed by his neck, chest, arms, legs and thighs, and finally his feet. A tear rolled down his cheek as he prayed that he would remain strong and not give his tormentors the satisfaction of hearing him scream. *I must be strong. I will be strong.*

Evil World functioned on the commands of a lunatic turned computer scientist; turned twisted medical doctor. Everyone called him *the Major*, but God only knows what his real name may have been.

He was tall and gaunt, with wisps of hair going in all directions, his eyes bulging from their sockets. His clothes were expensive but worn. Although no longer young, he was surprisingly agile and engaged. He loved his work.

Where do such men come from? What in God's name is going on? William thought to himself.

"It is good to see that you came of your own free will," the voice echoed, "no shackles, chains, not even handcuffs. I think that says a lot about your character."

William continued to stare straight ahead; he would not give *them* the satisfaction of turning his head to see hypodermic needles on the tray beside him. "Thanks…but it's not like I had a choice."

"My son, there are always choices and you chose to come here like a man. I admire that. The court sentenced you to death, but they didn't tell you how you would die or at what particular time your life would end," the voice responded.

"Allow me to welcome you to *Evil World*." He spread his arms and turned in a circle, " ... the gateway to the last place you will dwell. You will be trained. Through *Evil World*, you will assist in controlling the *Real World*. Above all remember this...," he said as he leaned down over Williams's reclining body and pinioned head, nose-to-nose with William. "There is but one rule ... In *Evil World*, there are no rules".   He laughed quietly.

"I wish we had more time, but an opening is about to occur. Although new, I believe that with your desire to achieve, you are the best candidate for the job. Unfortunately, you will not get the normal orientation to *EW*. I believe you will catch on quickly, and in a few months, you will graduate to a new life. So, let's get to work."

The IV was deftly inserted into his left arm and William went to sleep. Hours later, he awoke. He was still in the chair. Lying flat, his head felt like it had been blown to bits and re-assembled using a giant hammer to beat the parts into place. Slowly, he opened his eyes. The room was dim; he wasn't sure if it was day or night.

"Welcome back," the withered voice of the old man greeted him. "You've been out for a week, but a lot has been accomplished. Your desire to exceed expectations allowed us to complete months of programming in days. We can now plug you into the simulator and start your training."

The old man showed William a series of three plugs ... then inserted them into different parts of his skull. William flinched, and groaned, but determined to keep hold of himself, he did not scream or cry out.

"Very good: These will come in and out while you are trained. Afterward, permanent implants will be used and you won't feel a thing." The old man laughed.

William was in a sitting position. Eyes wide, he watched as the old man sat twisting knobs and pulling levers. William's head began to buzz, his body stiffened and he blacked out.

Months passed. The mad doctor kept pumping data and skills into William's head. He learned how to remain conscience during the sessions and respond in appropriate ways to various stimuli. William learned that when he did well by cooperating with the doctor, he got better food; even though he took nourishment intravenously, he could tell the difference in quality. The physical gifts provided by various assistants were quite enjoyable.

William knew that in the real world, he would never receive such attention. He also learned how to retain the experiences that traveled through his nervous system to his brain and relive them over and over again.

In time, he didn't require external stimuli to produce a memory; he simply continued to enjoy it. He convinced the assistants to perform daring forms of pleasure with his guidance. He claimed it stimulated him in order to operate at peak performance for the Doctor.

He also decided his mind was superior not only to those who had gotten him into trouble, but to those currently training and caring for him. To prove his point, he used his mind to get the more simple-minded staff to do small *favors* for him. He was never blatant or got anyone into trouble. He was growing stronger and gaining more control over his environment.

"William, my boy…do you feel ready to try out what you have learned?" the Doctor asked.

The screen, attached to William's brain, flashed *yes*. William could speak, but he knew it impressed the good doctor when he responded electronically.

"I am proud of you my boy; you have accomplished in less than six months what most of your predecessors never learned. This is your first true adventure outside the lab. Mind your manners and do the tasks you have been taught."

Translucent tubes snacked from his body to a new machine that tethered William. Images whirled in his mind and he immediately took charge of the information. He realized he was controlling the *Real World, with his mind* … transferring information, power, directions—everything. He was the fabric of the universe. William loved it and his mind continued to magnify.

He performed beyond expectation—learning to distinguish day from night, coordinating world activities, identifying and correcting problems throughout the grid. He still found time for small acts of personal satisfaction. He was giddy with his new-felt power.

Violently, William was jerked back from his virtual world and returned to the physical world. His body jerked, as if punched, but there was no pain. One second, he was master of the world, the next he was strapped to the same recliner, held captive by the doctor.

"You are ready, William. Despite your youth, I am placing you at the top of the pyramid. You will be the Chief Controller of *Real World.*

In this world, unlike the last, you can excel. It is expected and required that you do your best at all times. You will be monitored, and I will provide direction. Should you fail, you will no longer be a part of the vast universe of *Real World.* Those who fail are disconnected.

"I only have one warning, if you are disconnected, you will die. I suggest you do your job, and do it well."

"Yes sir … I will follow the rules. I need to know something.

"What is it William?"

"What is your name?" The question flashed on the screen.

The old man cocked his head to the left, smiled and said "Moriarty ... Dr. Moriarty."

The guards appeared once again. William's head was no longer restricted. Neither were his arms or legs; there was no need. After months of non-use, his muscles were like jelly. He couldn't raise himself from the chair, let alone run.

"Hello boys, good to see you again." William joked. His voice was gruff from lack of use.

Without response, the guards pushed William to an area far from the lab. They entered a large warehouse, filled with recliners; each held a person attached to wires and equipment. "Okay, wise guy. Here's where you live and sometime in the future, die." One of the guards said.

A woman wearing a lab coat, with a nametag that said "Betty," began hooking him to the mainframe of a giant computer. He was on a platform and had an unobstructed view of the entire facility.

"Welcome, sir. I'm one of many Betty's who will care for your physical needs. We will keep you clean, fed, and cared for, as long as you take care of the outside world.

'We can reward you for excellent work by providing high quality nutrients and stimulants. We are skilled in providing your physical body with various forms of relaxation and pleasure.

"If you don't do your job, we are equally skilled in pain. We find causing pain amusing. We can get authorization to disconnect you if you become lax in your responsibilities or anger us." With those words, William was plugged in, a cognitive cog in the wheel of *Evil World*.

He learned that his superior brain gave him the opportunity to review and forward every bit of information flowing through the multiple computer complexes. William was connected to multiple complexes filled with people trapped in an electronic prison. His orders allowed the *Real World* to operate as a coordinated unit.

He realized that through his hard work and ambition, he was at the very top of the food chain. He ran the world. There were others, like him, but less powerful. They were attached to him. They could request and suggest action, but they were conduits to provide him with information or to execute his commands.

In time, he became strong ... stronger than his old foes, the football players that used to beat him up at school. He was no longer the wimpy, awkward boy of the past, but a powerful entity.

He knew he was being monitored. *They don't even realize my power*. He observed, then memorized the cycles of monitoring and was aware when the unknown faces of those in charge, tapped into his brain. They not only reviewed his performance, but also dug deep into the recesses of his mind to try to discover his private thoughts and feelings.

They believed they could access his innermost thoughts. They were wrong. He had plans. To William, this was a game. Did they think that because he didn't obey the status quo in the *Real World* that he would sit still and become a computer chip now?

It took months, perhaps years. William wasn't sure of how much time had passed. Time stood still in *Evil World … his* world. He began diverting energy to his body, making it physically stronger. He expanded his mind by taking over parts of the minds of those below him. William compressed concepts, abilities, and powers in the minds of his subjects.

He maintained his secret—there would be a day when he was ready—then, and only then, would he strike.

There were pleasures to this life, he thought. He loved to locate his old enemies, the ones who made his life a living hell when he had a functioning body.

Accidents happened sometimes that even William, as the "Controller", had no power to change. After all, everyone dies from something and when a person's time is up…it is up. William simply reset their clocks.

Others were rewarded—friends, parents, and teachers. Those who treated him with kindness quietly received promotions or rewards that made their lives easier.

William even found the Doctor in the outside world and provided him with recognition for his work in improving lives of the living.

At last, William was ready. By his command, all the Betty's were sent somewhere in the warehouse—each called to the far corners of the building, away from his chair.

He was no longer restrained. His body, which had been too weak to support its own weight or move on its own, was now strong. He had flooded his body with nutrients, stimulating his muscles.

William commanded his mental unit to disconnect from his brain and body. Alarms did not sound as he continued to control the facility through wireless connections.

You've got to love Wi-Fi.

He still controlled the world and now he had control of himself too. Under his own power, he slowly staggered to the exit; as he opened the door, he gave the command for all those connected to him to shut down.

Through his link, he could hear the cries for help. The Bettys were overwhelmed by the failing operators. Services in the real world began to shut down.

Power, water, all modern conveniences ground to a halt. *Evil World* also began to die as the various *carbon based* computers ceased to function.

William walked with a heavy, labored stride to the lab that had made him the master of *Evil World*. He reached the laboratory door and opened it. Dr. Moriarty had a new person hooked up to the machines.

"Training my replacement, Doctor?" William asked. His words blinked in bright red on the screen above the doctor's head.

Moriarty whipped around to see William slowly shuffling towards him. Stunned, the doctor backed away muttering, "Not possible. It's not possible."

"Oh ... it's possible. Believe your eyes. At this very moment, the world you created is dying. You gave me control and I have shut it all down." William spoke with the gravelly voice caused by lack of use. His words appeared on the screen for dramatic effect.

The doctor moved to a switch on the wall. "I will shut you down. I warned you ..." he said as he threw the switch marked *command center*. Nothing happened.

William slowly continued walking towards the doctor. He smiled, knowing he had regained his humanity and that he had won. The human race had won.

"Not to worry Doc...you can't hurt me, I'm a dead man walking."

William continued his advance, "but before I go, just know I have shut down your entire system; I have eliminated all your carbon based computer modules and have placed this facility on lockdown.

All life support will end in thirty seconds; you will have two hours to think about what you have done to destroy the lives of achievers. I could have completed this task at my station but I wanted to say goodbye in person."

"This can't happen." The doctor screamed. "There are firewalls; there are programs ... there ... there, there are rules."

Smiling, William touted, "Ah doctor ... you forget ... in *Evil World*, there are no rules!"

Little Miss Moffett's Worst Nightmare

Every child remembers the nursery rhyme.

Little Miss Moffett,
Sat on a toffet,
Eating her curds and whey.
Along came a spider,
And sat down beside her
... and she squashed it with her spoon.

The poem ends, but the end of the story was never reported publicly. Little Miss Moffett went inside to wash the spoon so she could finish her curds and whey.

The spider, Toby, was splattered and spread across the ground. His cousin Gary had witnessed the killing and ran home to tell the grownups.

Moffett's problem was she messed with the wrong family. Toby came from a long line of royalty. This particular family of tarantulas lived in caves and caverns high in the mountains. They were larger than most tarantulas—much larger. As individuals they were fierce hunters, but together, in mass, they were formidable, and stalked anything breathing air.

Word of Toby's death spread throughout the kingdom. When word reached Queen Janice, she fainted. Toby was her baby; he was the six thousand-four-hundred-eighty first son in line to replace the king.

King Henry took the news calmly. He sat on his rock and slowly consumed a mouse as he thought about what had happened to his son. Toby should not have gone into the valley of humans. He entered their realm and paid the ultimate price ... but his death could not go unpunished. That would give the humans thoughts of invading King Henry's lands. That could never be allowed to happen.

Finished with his meal, King Henry tossed the husk aside and stood tall upon his rock. "Call the counsel to order. Prepare the armies of Arachnid. Alert the other kingdoms. We are at war!"

Within hours, the council members stood before the King. "A human has killed my son Toby. The thousand-eyed witness report describes a cold-blooded murder. We shall avenge Toby's death!" The counsel cheered.

The great army assembled as the sun set on the mountaintop. A living, creeping brown carpet flowed from the cavern entrance towards the valley.

There was no lack of food along the way. As the army made its way through human territory, it devoured any living creature that crossed its path. Progress was slow, as factions of this great gathering fed on bugs, birds, and larger animals.

A ravenous, leggy carpet of unrelenting mouths moved closer to its destination. They numbered half a million—some weighed over ten ounces and marching made them hungry.

By mid-afternoon of the third day, King Henry halted his troops at the edge of the forest. Moffett's hut was just ahead. The King sent scouts to explore the parameter, searching for ways to attack.

Suddenly a door opened and a young girl stepped into the yard. She tossed a large pillow, which landed on the flat surface of a large rock and then sat down and began to eat.

The King knew from the description that this was Moffett, the creature that had killed his son.

Henry seized the opportunity. He divided his troops into two groups. The first squadron headed towards the open door while Henry, along with the remaining divisions rushed the girl.

Moffett looked up from her bowl and saw the carpet of spiders racing towards her. She screamed in terror, throwing her bowl at them in desperate hope that it would repeal the advancing nightmare.

Mrs. Moffett stepped into the doorway to see what had caused her daughter to scream. That was the opportunity they had been looking for.

A squadron of hairy, thick bodies, and curved, disjointed legs poured across the threshold, climbed the outer wall and flooded onto the landing. Her feet were covered in seconds. She freaked, stomping her feet—popping sounds accompanied by unspeakable ooze covered the small porch.

King Henry's troops were skilled. Armed with a natural ability to jump, they attacked the woman's legs and soon gained new territory on her dress.

Fangs blazing, they bit deep into her bare skin. Several dropped from the top of the doorframe onto her head. Mrs. Moffett spun in place, frantic to beat the creatures away. Arms flailing about, she clamped her mouth shut least the beasts invade her inner parts.

Little Miss Moffett stood tiptoe on the rock attempting to push the creatures back to the ground as they swarmed over her.

Losing her footing on the slick, gut covered surface of the rock, Moffett landed face down on the ground. She was veiled by the biting hoards.

Screaming at the site of her fallen daughter, Mrs. Moffett charged out the door only to be silenced by the attacking spiders that had found their way into her mouth, biting, and choking her as she joined her daughter face down in the dirt.

Both females let loose blood curdling screams as thousands of fangs pumped vile poison into their skin. They tried to fend off the furry foes, but were hopelessly outnumbered. In an instant, both females looked like fallen logs, covered in brown, undulating bark.

Within the hour, mother and daughter lay still in the dirt, buried under thousands of spiders, gorging themselves on the fluids that had once given life to their bodies.

It took several hours for the troops to feed. However, by nightfall the bodies like spent husks, lay dry and empty as locus shells. The army formed ranks and headed home as King Henry rejoiced in his victory.

The King estimated that he had lost at least fifty thousand troops—acceptable losses. They had won, the humans were dead and Toby was avenged. The army disappeared into the underbrush.

That evening, Mr. Moffett arrived home and discovered the shelled remains of his wife and daughter. He surveyed the ground and knew who had killed his family. The bodies of the heinous killers littered the yard—some of the eight-legged devils still clung to the bodies of his wife and daughter.

He ran to the village. Other men returned with him to examine the carnage and helped him bury his family.

Hate burned in his heart as he looked towards the mountains. "We have lived in peace for centuries, now they come to our land and kill our families. They will pay, and pay dearly," he cried to the heavens.

It took four days for the men to organize and gather all that would be required to attack the Spider

King. Men from other villages joined the hunt fearing their homes would be next. They gathered at the Moffett home and brought with them a variety of oil and poisons.

For days they conferred, and conspired with one another on how to launch their counter assault. They knew the spiders, if attacked, would remain, and defend their mountain home. The assembled army of men slowly climbed the mountain. They saw many spiders along the way.

Men and spiders had interacted in the valley for hundreds of years. They had maintained a tense but peaceful existence where men farmed the lands and spiders ate harmful insects.

Now all had changed. The men, united in revenge, climbed with purpose. Their mission—to enter the cave and destroy the creatures. They killed every spider that fell within their reach during the march.

The tarantulas that did escape the human army did not bother to spread the word to King Henry. Life and death were always a part of living among men.

The next afternoon, the village men stood at the opening of the cavern. "Spider," Mr. Moffett commanded, "Show yourself."

He and the others made their way into the cave. Spiders watched them from their hidden places. A few spiders attempted to tell the king that the humans had entered their cave, but those tarantulas were killed before they could escape the light of the torches.

The men moved deeper into the cave. They spaced themselves across the opening as they walked, spreading poison and other chemicals along the walls and the ground. At last, they arrived before the throne of King Henry.

Henry calmly sat on his rock watching with his many eyes, assuming the humans had come to his realm to beg for forgiveness and proclaim a peace between the Arachnid and the human.

The king's subjects were not so comfortable with the men entering their kingdom. They formed lines of protection.

"We have arrived," one of the men said. They formed teams and began to spray chemicals on the floor, walls, and ceiling of the cave. Other men rolled containers deeper into the cave that spread liquid among the homes and nests of the spiders.

The spiders looked to King Henry—on his word they would attack without mercy. The men began stepping on the lines of insects covering the floor. Their boots protected them from bites. Many of the spiders felt dizzy, the noxious fumes of the liquid were killing them.

The men had covered their boots with toxic chemicals. Soon the nests were covered with poison that flowed into the innermost darkness that was King Henry's empire.

Henry continued to watch, at first he was amused by this show of worship. He saw no reason to fear the humans or to tell his army to attack. It was when he heard the screams of his family and followers as they died that he realized his error.

Henry gave the order to attack but it was too late. The wall of poison was formidable.

King Henry was no longer amused and bared his fangs. One of the humans threw the torch near his throne. Oil burst into flames. King Henry felt the heat and found his feet were stuck to the rock. He cooked in seconds.

Heat and smoke filled the cavern. The humans turned and ran towards the entrance, spraying the walls behind them. The cavern was alive with fire. The men threw bottles filled with a flammable liquid; they shattered against the walls of the cave, spreading the flames onto the ceiling, walls and floor.

As the men ran out the cave entrance, they sprayed behind them. The air grew hot and toxic, exploding, and spewing its deadly gases out the cave opening.

The entrance collapsed in seconds as the explosion brought down tons of rock and dirt. "Let them roast and die in agony for what they have done to my family," Moffett yelled in victory.

High above the cavern, the remnant of spiders watched as the humans began to walk down the hill. Their numbers were small, only a few hundred or so remained of the great colony. Unlike men, spiders think as one. They stood in silent thought as they watched the murderers retreat.

We will build a new colony. We will find these men and their families and destroy them, and their offspring. We will not rest until it is done. King Henry will be avenged, and then men will be no more.

The men of the valley shall rue the day
Of chasing, and killing the spiders in sway.

With fury and hunger for revenge so sweet,
Spiders shall have all the humans to eat.

And so it shall be, for the sons of men
  ... That the fang and the fur shall avenge
  their great sin.

The Gift

Charlie sat, alone in the dining room. The soft candlelight set the mood as quiet music played in the background. The flowers he had purchased that afternoon filled the room with the smell of spring.

Her anniversary gift sat at the opposite end of the table—a small box, wrapped in red metallic paper wrapped in a gold ribbon. It sat alone, carefully positioned in the center of her salad plate.

Bet she forgot, again. Charlie thought, *I don't know why I keep trying. After twelve years, you would think I would learn.*

Still, he waited another hour; the candles burned down to nubs, smoky black wax veins marred the once smooth surface. He turned on the overhead light and ate in silence. When he had eaten his fill, he put her meal in the microwave, walked into the den and poured a drink.

He drank several drinks that night. When he made his way to bed—in the guest room, it was well after midnight.

Stella arrived home just before dawn. She always took advantage of Charlie's out-of-town trips. She felt alive and young again. She realized her life had been wasted during the faithful years of her marriage. It wasn't until her friend Brenda invited her out one weekend while Charlie was out of town that she realized how out of touch she was with having fun. The hottest clubs in L.A. offered her a buffet of dancing partners who were never shy about trying to turn her on.

She teased her partners, yet never truly cheated on her husband until the night she met the young lifeguard. She went home with him and discovered that the excitement and thrill of sex with a stranger opened up a new world of pleasure. After that, she took advantage of every moment good old Charlie was on a business trip.

Stella enjoyed all the young men that vied for her attention. Of course, she paid their way. They were young and broke, she on the other hand, was older and very secure financially. In return, the boys left her physically satisfied and taught her ways of pleasure that she had never dreamed of or tried in her youth.

The smell of food, candle wax, and the light in the dining room told her that Charlie had been home last night. *He's been home all night. He knows that I have been out for hours.*

Her first thought was the prenup. She couldn't let a night of fun and passion blow her financial security with Charlie. She needed a cover story and it had to be believable. She might even have to get down to bare skin and distract him.

It was when she headed to the kitchen for coffee and to get her story straight, that she saw the box, still nestled on the plate. She grabbed the box and the note underneath as she passed through the swinging door. She poured the coffee, and after her first good swallow, she picked up the note.

It was short, "Happy Anniversary. Dinner is in the zapper. L ... Charlie." She looked in the microwave and decided it might have been a good dinner several hours ago but now it was just something for the trash.

She picked up the box and thought, *Yup, the old boy spent big bucks for this anniversary. Bet he was hoping to get lucky. He just might.* That way she might not have to explain why she wasn't home or why she didn't have a gift for him.

He could forgive her forgetting their anniversary; it wasn't her fault that he was home three days early. She would have to put something together so it would look like she had planned a surprise. No getting around it—she would have to buy the old bastard a nice gift.

She opened the box and found a small card that read: *The gift that keeps on giving to the one I love.* Under the tissue was a ring. A blood red ruby anchored in the center, encircled by a ring of diamonds and a second ring of small, black stones. *The ruby and chocolate diamonds must have cost a fortune.*

The ring was light considering the size and number of stones. Stella knew jewelry, and even though she didn't know the value of the chocolate diamond's she knew the ring had set Charlie back six figures. *He was making more money than he was telling.*

He must not be too mad, she thought; *he left the ring for me to find.* With a smile, she slipped the ring on her finger; it was a perfect fit.

Stella made her way upstairs and was surprised that Charlie was not in bed. She showered, and slid naked between the sheets and went to sleep.

Morning came and went before Stella got out of bed. Charlie was gone, but there was a note on the kitchen counter.

> *Sorry, darling. I should have told you I was coming home for our anniversary. I know how involved you are with your political projects. I should have phoned ahead to let you know. Forgive my being so irresponsible. I have some business to finish up out of town and I'll be gone for five days. Sorry we missed our evening together. I hope you like your gift.*
>
> *Love always,*
> C

Stella couldn't believe her luck. She was out cheating and he was apologizing for not letting her know he was coming home. Under the circumstances, she decided allow him to give her a full body massage when he returned.

Following her regular routine, Stella showered, went to the gym, and ate a light lunch with a couple of friends where they had a good laugh over Charlie. After lunch, she returned home, napped, then prepared for a night of partying and being pleasured by young men with no brains but plenty of staying power.

Stella arrived at *Wet n Wild* about ten in the evening. She was a regular, so getting in the club wasn't a problem. Slightly older than the most of the clientele, Stella had worked hard to seduce the managers and guarantee her name on the admit list. It didn't matter that it cost a fifteen-minute service every couple of weeks to stay on the lists. It was worth it. Besides, the owner spread the word to other A-list clubs about Stella's skilled tongue and sharp nails, which put her name on other admission lists and VIP rooms. It helped that she had the body of a woman half her age—thanks to Charlie's money and her expensive personal trainer. Her plastic surgery didn't hurt either.

Stella found a spot at the end of the bar and began the hunt. It was easy to snatch a stud from the young girls. First, find the target, buy him a drink and let the cash flow. Second, a bit of dirty dancing and in less than an hour, step three, you were in a no-tell hotel for a romp. Wear him out, then go to another bar and do the same thing.

She didn't need or desire a relationship, this was for the adventure. Sleeping with men half her age invigorated her. She loved it. It made her feel alive, desirable.

Stella was skilled and knew what she wanted. In less than an hour, she and her first stud were naked and sweaty in a cheap hotel. He had worn out early. He was a bodybuilder—lots of muscle but no staying power. His lack of stamina was something she hadn't counted on. *These young guys, they just aren't what they used to be*, she thought.

The bodybuilder slept with a slight smile on his lips, satisfied with his personal performance and overwhelmed by Stella's.

She looked down at him with a cold fury she couldn't identify. It had never bothered her if she picked up an inadequate lover; she simply went out to find another. Tonight, it was different. *How dare he sleep while I am still unsatisfied, I'll show him.*

Quietly, she got out of bed and cut the ropes from the window blinds. He was tied hand and foot when she woke him.

"Hey Stud," she whispered in his ear. "I've got a proposition for you. Satisfy me or die." She climbed on top of him, wrapped a piece of cord around his neck, and began to pull the ends.

Later, she woke from a restless nap and discovered his dead body next to her. The cord around his neck had tightened, splitting the skin on his neck. She was covered with blood, but it didn't bother her. She noticed her ring; it sparkled as if it had its own energy supply—untarnished by the mess.

As if she were dreaming, Stella calmly got up, showered, dressed, and made her way to another club. By dawn, she had visited two more clubs. She had taken three lovers in one night and left three dead bodies.

The sun had just cleared the horizon when she walked into her house and went straight to bed. Hours later, she awoke. The bed was soaked in sweat. It was the terrible nightmare. It took several minutes for Stella to calm herself. The dream seemed so real, the sex so sweet, but it was the blood she remembered most vividly. She remembered it as sweet, sticky, and satisfying—like a craving of some kind, a hunger that she had never known.

She thought of Charlie and for the first time in years, she missed him. She felt hollow without him, anxious. *Why doesn't he come home and take care of me?* It was a strange feeling, missing Charlie. She wasn't sure why she missed him or how he could quiet her distress, but she needed him to be there. Her dreams disturbed her. She needed relief, only the relief that Charlie could give her.

Stella put the dream out of her mind and continued her regular routine. She found herself at the gym, working out and thinking about the adventures she had planned for the evening. Perhaps an earlier start would help her find satisfaction. She was hungry for the release that only sex with a stranger could give her. She thought of some of the more exotic clubs in town and decided to wear leather.

She had a constant nagging and realized she wanted Charlie, but he wouldn't be back for a few more days. For the first time she could remember, she actually needed Charlie. She decided she would give him a welcome home that he wouldn't soon forget.

Maybe this nightlife isn't all it is cracked up to be, she thought. *I need Charlie.* She loved him and it was time she gave him her attention. She would again become the faithful wife, only now, better trained to encourage Charlie to take her with him on his business trips.

Her intentions were good. She wanted to stay home and stop the craziness, but she couldn't stop. She became a woman possessed as she showered, worked out, and went clubbing, but with the sunrise, she had the nagging feeling that something was wrong. She felt guilty and the longing for her husband was becoming unbearable.

On the fifth morning, Stella caught the news on one of the televisions at the gym. A serial killer was stalking young men in the club districts. Photos of the victims flashed across the screen. Stella stopped the stair master. Each of the faces reminded her of someone she had seduced. The descriptions of their deaths were like her nightmares.

Sick to her stomach, she wondered if someone had seen her in those clubs with all those dead men; the security cameras would have her picture.

Oh, God, what am I going to do? What if the police come after me? How can I explain to Charlie what has happened?

Charlie would be back tonight. She went straight to the house and got ready for him. They would talk and he would help her figure out what was going on in her head. He had to help her.

It was late afternoon when Charlie walked through the door. Stella charged him, kissed him, and showed him the affection he had never experienced, but had always longed for. Stella had never been this passionate toward her husband, not even on their honeymoon. "Missed you too," he whispered in her ear as she pushed him onto the couch pleasing the two of them.

Later, they sat, had drinks, a light dinner and made love a third time. Charlie enjoyed himself. He did things she never allowed him to do in the past. He sensed her need for him and he decided to take advantage of it. It was about time he got something out of this relationship besides a thinner wallet.

What he found interesting was that none of the new positions or techniques seemed new to her. She even gave him directions to make it *more fun*.

It was in the early morning hours when she poured them a drink, looked directly into his eyes and said, "We need to talk."

"Okay." He set his drink on the coffee table and settled in, wondering what she might say.

"Charlie, I have a problem. I'm having dreams — vivid, frightening dreams. I don't remember when it started, but I have been having these nightmares and I just discovered that each dream involves a real person. I saw on the news that several men are dead, and I have had dreams, nightmares really, about all of them. I'm scared that it has something to do with me," she said crying.

"Interesting," said Charlie, "Let's have another drink and talk about it some more." Charlie poured the drinks. An imperceptible smile caught the corner of his mouth for an instant. *Life is good and about to get better, for me. She has never needed me before.*

He turned back to Stella and listened carefully. He asked questions about the news and her dreams, exacting detail after detail. She didn't tell him how she knew the murdered men nor did she mention her indiscretions.

At dawn, she rewarded his concern with another wild romp. It was over breakfast when he told her he was going out of town again. It was only for a couple days. "I will try to have some answers for you when I get back. I need to talk to a friend of mine."

That afternoon, he left. Stella paced the house, determined to stay home and fight her desires. As the evening came on she was nervous, and distracted. She decided to take a shower. *No harm in that. I can take a shower and relax, maybe fall asleep* Two hours later she was at the club.

The next morning she was startled awake. Sitting up, she realized she was covered in sweat. She looked up and stifled a scream. Sitting in the chair across the room was Charlie.

"Morning Lovely," he said calmly, "did you have a busy night?"

He had a local news station playing on the bedroom television. The reporter was vividly describing another murder. Stella whispered, "Oh god ... my dreams."

"No love. Never dreams, those are flashbacks," he said.

"Flashbacks? What do you mean?" She stared at her husband in shock. A quiet cough caused her to turn her head to the bedroom door. Shocked by Charlie's comment, she jumped when she saw a stranger standing in her bedroom. She was naked, but didn't bother to cover herself.

"Oh, let me introduce you to Dr. Johnson. The good doctor runs an inpatient clinic in Canada; I think you should spend some time there."

"It's simple, my dear, I met the good doctor a year or so ago. We discussed my intimacy problems and he felt that the problem wasn't me but you."

Charlie explained that he had been suspicious of her for over two years, and that he had hired a private investigator. "You have always been indifferent towards me, but about two years ago you suddenly went cold. You ignored me, Stella. You forgot the words "thank you." You demanded and took, and I gave. I knew something was going on."

Charlie leaned forward and placed his hand on the edge of the bed. "That's why I had you followed. You do live in two worlds, don't you? You are the rich, cold, selfish wife and a hot wild party girl." He smiled at her and the smile froze her heart.

"After my discoveries, I had several discussions with the doctor. At his suggestion, I continued to be the faithful husband, not noticing that you were never home, or involved with me. I always gave you an out. Our anniversary was the crowning touch. At the good doctor's suggestion, I continued to play along until he had your therapy prepared."

"Therapy?" She felt weak.

"He's a unique specialist. He made your ring and it won't come off unless you cut off your finger. It magnifies your lusts. But … it does something more. It causes your unfulfilled lust to turn to rage. Murderous rage. Your wild liaisons become a blood bath because the ring feeds off all the negative energy. Its power grows when covered in blood. It then turns your lust into relentless guilt. The only person who can satisfy your unquenchable lust is the person who gave you the ring—me."

Charlie looked at Stella. "The need to fill the emptiness with more lust and violence forces you to continue the cycle, it is never ending. You will never be satisfied and you will keep on killing. Eventually, the authorities will catch you. Unfortunately, this state does not believe in capital punishment. Because of your violent nature, you will spend all your time in solitary confinement driven far beyond crazy with desires you can't fill. In the end, you will take your own life." He rubbed his hands together and smiled, as if he had just finished a good meal.

"The best part, my love, is that it doesn't matter if you never cheat on me again, you will have the dreams for the rest of your life, and each time they will become more vivid, and more detailed. In time, the dreams will be with you every moment. You will relive every romp and murder that has put you where you are today. Your only moments of sanity, if you can call it that, will be when you are fulfilling your lust for sex or violence with a new victim."

"Charlie, you can't do this to me. I am your wife."

Charlie continued. "Oh, I did mention you could cut of your finger to be rid of the ring, but should that happen, the dreams and lust will intensify beyond the limits of sanity."

Stella couldn't move. He was a monster. How could she not have seen the evil hiding within him?

"You do have one escape. If you go to the clinic, Dr. Johnson will be able to control the dreams through very special therapy. You can feed your lust with his staff, special guests and select patients. He will keep you from killing, most of the time and the medication will keep you from going completely mad."

Stella's sobs racked her naked body.

"I may visit once in a while to help calm your nerves." He ran his fingertips along her collarbone, "or you may not see me while I simply stay in the background and watch you perform. It's your choice, stay home and be caught by the police, or admit yourself to the clinic and find some semblance of peace."

Stella was admitted to the clinic. Her hungers were controlled but never satisfied. Her desires grew as she descended deeper into an abyss of lust and violence. There were bodies, always bodies as Dr. Johnson realized that Stella enjoyed killing. The good doctor was able to establish a clientele specifically to meet her needs. She killed those who needed killing — crime lords, racketeers, corrupt politicians, and others.

The institute also eliminated dangerous people for governments, for a fee. The victims were always given the terms of survival; satisfy Stella and live. No one survived.

The dreams continued. Stella remained in a state of constant need for lust and blood. Her sleep was drug induced. Her life became a never-ending cycle of lust, violence, shame, and hate.

Charlie was always there. He would stand in her cell and watch the action. He enjoyed talking to her when she was naked and covered in blood and it seemed to calm her nerves. He came to relish that moment when Stella realized what she had done and screamed for salvation. He watched the videos and listened to her screams as lust and horror engulfed her mind and body. Some nights he would play the sounds of her misery on speakers in her room. He became addicted to her pain.

Charlie and Doctor Johnson had a deal. They split the income from Stella's activities in half. He kept Stella but just for laughs.

From time to time, they recruited new women, equipped them with a ring, and then charged for their services. They found a new source of income, complete with videos of all the action.

One afternoon, the two men stood in front of six cells, watching through one-way glass. Cameras rolled as they watched six new subjects perform for their specialized brand of entertainment.

"My good Doctor, you were right, revenge is sweet. And I have to admit, the rings are gifts that keep on giving!"

Charlie smiled.

Dark Carnival

The Carnival arrived with the glitz and glamour of a burned out two-dollar hooker. The parade included two elephants with missing tusks, a tired, shaggy lion, clumsy jugglers who kept dropping their balls, a strong man with no muscle, a bearded lady with mange, and an assortment of oddities that would bring the locals to old man Potter's field for two exciting nights.

On Friday afternoon, the local farmers joined the carneys, putting up the main tent, as well as smaller tents for sideshows and games. Wagons were placed around the field; the animals were fed and watered. That night the lilt of the calliope and the calls of the side show pitchmen could be heard all over town. It didn't matter—everyone was at the carnival.

The outside acts began in the late afternoon. Performers wandered around the field doing simple tricks and inviting the crowd to the main tent for the big show that night.

The show began at 8:00 p.m. as the townspeople who had been milling around the field made their way to the main tent. Melody Clark, the sheriff's daughter led her eight-year-old sister into the *big top*.

Melody was brimming over with excitement and wonder. She and her sister had never been to a circus, but it seemed to Melody that as the evening's entertainment progressed, each act became more dark and scary.

Younger children began to cry, women became agitated, and grown men grew angry. The clowns, although full of antics, were off-putting. The animals looked at the audience as if they were a late night snack. The performers flirted with certain men and women during their performances, their eyes filled with hunger and the carneys seemed most interested in the children.

The show ended and as the people began to exit the tent a collective sigh seemed to run through the crowd. Once outside the tent in the light of the torches and fresh air, the evil of the circus seemed to pass from everyone's thoughts.

People milled around, their mouths stuffed with forbidden treats that were never served at home as they watched the sideshow attractions. They stood in line to ride the Merry Go Round and the Ferris wheel. The house of horrors was popular with young lovers and older children.

On Saturday evening, Melody once again escorted her younger sister to the carnival. Melody wished she could have left her sister at home so she could explore some of the more adult sideshows but her parents would not let her come alone. The rides were packed with families, kids, and single adults alike. The

Painted clowns that wandered about the circus grounds, still wore makeup from the previous night. It looked dirty ... evil.

Other performers made off-colored remarks to the women in the crowd. Some performers made obscene gestures and comments to the audience. Some of them refusing to perform their acts and instead, offering *special shows* to certain women and men in the stands in exchange for joining them in their tents.

Some of the people who were offended complained to the sheriff, but he said he was powerless. No crime was being committed.

The carnival shut down at midnight. The townspeople filed home to fall into a deep, dreamless sleep. Early the next morning, they awoke to discover that all of the children under the age of ten, along with several hundred head of cattle, pigs, and chickens were missing.

The sheriff and his deputies arrived at Potter's field to discover that the carnival had packed up and left during the night. Someone called the state police. They checked all the highways, but the caravan was nowhere to be found.

The police organized a systematic search. The town's people were lined up and spread across the field. They walked the entire area slowly making their way to the center of the field. As they walked, they searched for any kind of evidence that could explain what had happened to the children and the animals.

Evidence markers were placed at each location where a few tokens were discovered lying in the grass. The markers would later be used to help the sheriff's investigation. As the search continued, more sinister clues came to light.

Carved statues and coins, many made of gold, silver, and copper were scattered about the field. The coins were older than the history of the town. Most of the items dated back hundreds if not thousands of years. Broken pieces of equipment, tools, both modern and ancient, littered the area where the rides had been. A rotten white carousel horse lay broken, and half buried in the dirt.

By mid-morning, the searchers reached the center of the field where the big top had stood. They gasped. Scattered about was a series of piled ashes, some still smoldering. The ground was scorched and brittle, yet there was no smell of smoke. Bones littered the ground. "Well, we know what happened to our animals," someone said.

Others knelt, and began to scream as they lifted bones from the ash—not of animals, but bones of small humans—the remains of their children. The sheriff looked over the shoulders of those weeping on their knees.

"Oh God help us ... they were eaten ... cooked, and eaten. The carneys are gone. It's like the entire group has vanished," the sheriff whispered.

"They've gone back to hell," old man Potter shouted. "But don't worry, they'll be back ... they'll be back, in a hundred years or so." The crowd looked at the old man, not believing their ears.

Potter barked a hard, menacing laugh. He had everyone in his control. "Now forget all this, all of you ... return home, go about your lives, you will lose all memories of the children, their photos and personal possessions have already been removed. By dark, you won't even remember the little ones having been in your lives."

The people stared at Potter; he was no longer old but young and vibrant ... full of life. Potter jumped into the tractor seat. His plow began to bury the evidence, along with the memories of the weekend.

One by one, the people made their way home. They were like dream walkers.

All evidence of the missing children had been removed. As the day continued, all thoughts of the children left their minds. By nightfall, the entire town would return to the routine of living their daily lives. The children forgotten—erased.

Potter smiled. It wasn't a bad pact he had struck with *Old Nick*. He had been stuck in this county for over 600 years but still, not a bad life.

He wetted his lips as he thought of young Melody Clark. She had helped with the search in her tight shorts with her shirt tied just under her young jutting breasts. Yes, she would be his next wife. She would serve him well and learn the ways of darkness. When he grew tired of her, he would commit her soul to the dark and her body to his stomach. He could trade her for a hot replacement; or he might choose one of the girls taken the last time the circus came town. He might ask for Victoria, who had been the devil's plaything for the last hundred years. '*By now, she will have learned tricks that even I haven't thought of.*' Perhaps in another few hundred years, Melody could rejoin him after the demons and Satan himself had taught her what it means to obey and please a master.

No sir, this wasn't such a bad life. There was much to do as the town and the county continued to grow. He would continue to encourage the not-so-pure activities of the people, just to keep life interesting. It makes souls easier to claim the next time—when the circus comes to town.

Hell Found Me

Hell found me, and I didn't know I was lost ...

Saturday mornings gave me time to think about my past, present and future. My life was never easy and often unpleasant. However, the past ten years had been different; they had brought me happiness.

I had been divorced for twelve years and had managed to get myself out of debt and move to a new town. Thanks to a promotion and long hours at my own restaurant, I was making excellent money. Life was good.

Then Hell found me. I was in a small used bookstore. I heard someone call my name. "Hey Simon; What 'cha doing?"

Yup, I recognized that screech. I would know it anywhere.

I didn't bother to smile and in my most sarcastic voice, I said, "Well, I'm not ordering a pizza."

I returned to the bookshelves, hoping she would take the hint. She didn't. Out of the corner of my eye, I watched as she made her way down the aisle, headed straight for me.

She stopped dead in front of me, her hands resting on her shapely hips, a smirk on her glossy lips. She tossed her long black hair away from her face. *God, she looks younger than ever*, I thought to myself. "Well, aren't you even going to say hello?" The whine of her voice made my blood boil. I could see my hands gleefully wrapped around her throat, squeezing as her face turned blue while she bit her tongue and her eyes popped out.

"I told you in court, I have nothing more to say to you and never want to see you again. So, in the interest of maintaining a pleasant day, why don't you just walk away and return to the fiery pit of hell that sent you here."

"Ah come on, Simon, it's been a lo-o-o-o-ng time, and time wounds all heels, or something like that … can't we be friends?"

"Look Amy, we got divorced for a reason … I can't stand you … you got the house, car, and half the bank account. I got one hundred percent of the bills. So, no, we can't be friends, and by the way; how did you find me?"

"Oh, that was easy. Remember Tom Hardy from HR, well, with the help of a little small talk and a locked office door; he gladly told me where you transferred. A brief check of the company restaurants in this area, and as Sherlock Holmes always said, 'Elementary, my dear Watson.'"

I shook my head ... then wondered what she wanted with me. I did have to admit, she looked better now than she had ten years ago. Her well-maintained, tight body, belied her age. She must have had her bosom enlarged—from the looks of them, she had added a liter or two. No discernible graying in her hair and not a wrinkle on her face. *At forty you have the face you deserve, or the one you can afford,* I thought.

Before I could get lost in her charms, I reminded myself ... again. Beauty is skin deep ... but ugly goes clean to the bone. She was an evil woman. Believe me when I say that she was the essence of pure evil.

"Glad to hear about your newly acquired detective skills, but let's get on with it. What do you want? Surely in twelve years, you've found some other guy whose life you are making miserable."

She pouted, "How can you say such cruel things? What makes you think I want anything?" That one raised the old eyebrows.

"Okay, there is a small, tinsy favor I could use, that involves the two of us. Can we find a place where we can sit down and talk?"

My heart raced as I left the bookstore. At least she couldn't rip out my beating heart and eat it in public, could she? We walked to an outdoor coffee shop at the opposite end of the block and sat down. She ordered a fancy mixture of something that was high in calories and low in caffeine while I remained empty handed.

"You ordered it, you buy it ... I'm through paying your way." I snarled, "Now what do you want."

She batted her eyes, as she looked over the top rim her cup. "Well...I discovered something a few months ago, right after my most recent divorce. I don't think our divorce was ever finalized. My lawyer failed to file the papers with the court."

She smiled innocently as she continued, "Now, I figure you are happily married again and I don't want to ruin that for you." Her voice remained sweet, but her look could have frosted the glasses in every bar in town. "So ... if you will drive back to Dayton, re-file, and give me $20,000, I will get out of your life and no one will be the wiser."

I looked at her, shock registering on my face. Of course, I knew her attorney hadn't filed any papers because mine did. I was the one who petitioned for a way out of that *private hell* we called a marriage. She didn't know who had to file the paperwork after going to court.

She was wrong about one thing, I had never remarried, call me gun shy. I also knew that once black mailed, always black mailed. If I paid, she would never be out of my life.

"Tell you what, Amy, let me check with the court and see if this can be done without another divorce filing. In the meantime, let's sit down and talk things over so everything is agreed upon in case we do need to re-file." A simple plan began forming.

"Where are you staying? I can stop by work, pick up dinner for us, and bring it there. Now before you object, I don't want my past meeting my present. If you do something to make yourself known to my employees and friends, the deal is off."

She stared at me for a minute, not believing I had given in so quickly. "Call off the deal and the hell I gave you in our marriage will seem like a picnic compared to what I will do." I could almost see the smoking brimstone coming out of her ears. Some things never change.

"Look, I'm happy here. My life is simple and I want to keep it that way. If you start going all Gargoyles on me, it may be more than non-cooperation you'll get. Before you make threats, think about how publicity could change your life. Bigamy is illegal, plus, any money you got from any ex-husband will have to be returned. All I'm asking for is a bit of privacy. If I have to file again, fine, but I will add a clause stating you will never have direct or indirect contact with me again. It will be a built in restraining order that can't be revoked. Agreed?"

After making it perfectly clear that all I wanted was peace and quiet, not a war, she gave me her motel room number ... a cheap 'no-tell motel' just outside of town. We agreed on a time. She left and I went back to the bookstore. After completing a few hours of nonfiction research, I walked into work and prepared her a special meal.

I arrived at her room at exactly 6:30 p.m. with hot food, wine, and my best fake smile. I brought everything in with a wheeled catering cart that made it easy to include china, flatware, a linen tablecloth, and napkins.

Amy opened the door wearing a baby doll outfit from some adult bookstore or low-end lingerie shop. She was all sweet and sunshine as she invited me in and kissed me on the cheek.

I restrained myself from asking if our dinner was between tricks. No need fanning the flames of hell without good cause. I smiled and told her she looked good and proceeded to turn the pressed wood table into a banquet setting.

I opened a bottle of medium quality wine, and discovered that the wine glasses were broken in transit. She shrugged and said "Wine is good in a glass or right out of the box." She produced plastic glasses from the bathroom.

Since I no longer drink, I filled her cup and she swallowed the first eight ounces in one gulp. "Good stuff," she said as she refilled the glass.

"What's your plan, buddy, get me drunk and ravish me?" Her eyes flashed at the thought of telling the court how we had been together just before I re-filed.

I shook my head *no* and explained that I knew what she liked, and if we were going to discuss the details of our new arrangement, we might as well be comfortable.

I placed her dinner on the table. She admired the steak, cooked to perfection smothered with mushrooms and grilled onions, fresh peas floating in a heavy buttery sauce and cherry wine. I had prepared her favorite side dish, mashed potatoes, heaped with thick brown gravy. I opted for baked chicken, rice, and green beans. I included fresh baked French rolls, glazed with real butter, still warm from the oven.

She scowled at my plate. "Like I said, I've made a lot of changes, cleaned up my diet, gym, karate; I no longer drink or smoke. All I need to do is start going to church." I laughed.

She ate like a starving demon at a soul's buffet. As always, the potatoes and gravy were inhaled, mixed with the peas; she attacked the steak with her bare hands. I had forgotten what an animal she could be and was glad we were not in public.

"What else you got?" She demanded. I reached in the cart and removed a second, half-gallon container of potatoes and a quart of gravy, pint of peas, and uncovered a second thirty-two ounce steak. The built in plate warmer kept the steak hot, without overcooking it.

"You do know how to please a girl," she purred as she ate directly from the containers.

Throughout the meal, I made sure her wine glass was full. She was finishing the third bottle and she was still eating.

I went along with her demands offering only minor challenges from time to time. I made notes on a legal pad while she gorged herself.

By the end the cherry cheesecake, the fourth bottle sat empty on the floor beside her. Her plate and the extra containers were empty. She had room to finish my chicken and rice.

She leaned back in her chair, emitting a loud and juicy burp. She was, for once, satisfied.

"You always had a good appetite, Amy, how do you stay so thin?" I started to clean off the table and remove all of the evidence of my visit and of the meal she had eaten.

"I work out a lot," she laughed. "Actually, I tend to starve myself and puke when I eat too much ... but this was just too good. I will pay a price when I get back home. I'll spend extra time on the Stairmaster and in the sweatbox, and then get to the gym. You were always a good cook ... no matter what I said when we were together."

She carried her glass of wine to a nightstand and stretched out on the bed, her head propped up on all the pillows. "You know Simon, you are cooperating so well and that meal was out of site. I really expected one of our old screaming matches over this."

Her breasts were reaching for freedom, straining the thin baby doll top.

She sat up Indian style on the bed, making sure I got a good look at her long legs. "Why don't you come here and get a reward for being such a good boy," she slurred as she patted her thigh. "I've learned several new skills since the divorce. Who knows, we may decide to stay married and you move back to Dayton."

Nodding, I continued cleaning up. One thing I could say about Amy, she never let a crumb hit the floor. I left the wine bottles scattered around the room.

Packed and almost ready to leave, I looked at her. She was half conscience, leaning back on the pillows, still showing her perfect legs, but looking rather green. "What's the matter, Mistress of Satan, eat too much?"

Smiling I watched her try to respond. She could no longer lift her head. Gurgling sounds bubbled up from her mouth as the first bit of blood oozed down her chin.

I stood at the foot of the bed watching. A smile reached my eyes, and I realized that this was the first real joy I had felt since meeting her at the bookstore.

"In case you are wondering what's happening, I remembered your love of pain killers, so I loaded the peas with a special combination of numbing agents and other interesting chemicals. The potatoes were seasoned with a variety of strong painkillers. Of course, none of them mixes well with alcohol. You didn't feel it going down, and you won't feel anything as it continues to come up."

I rejoiced, "If the chemicals don't get you, you'll choke on your own blood."

She continued to gag. A seizure tightened her body like a board. She relaxed as I watched her eyes fade into a blank stare. I was amazed at the amount of blood, and partially chewed food covering her body and bed.

I reached into my pocket and opened two boxes of condoms and put some on the dresser, in her nightstand drawer, and placed a few empty wrappers on the floor after allowing her lifeless hand to open them.

The police will think she was on a binge and overdosed by accident. With her history of sex, drugs, and over indulgences, her death will be identified as an accidental suicide. "I'll admit to the police that she found me in the bookstore and we went to the coffee shop to talk. My story is that she wanted to get back together, but I wasn't interested." Smiling, I opened the motel door. No one was around. Removing the white server gloves, I headed for my car. If seen, I looked like just another traveler getting back on the road for parts unknown.

Yes... Hell had found me, but I found my redemption in the form of a good meal.

In Too Deep

What happened to you, Tommy? I can remember when you were a stand-up guy and could be trusted." The voice came from beyond the bright light shining in his eyes. He recognized that voice; he knew it, as if it was his own.

"Charlie ... Charlie. You have to believe me! I'm going to get you the money. I'm just a little short, that's all. I've had some problems the last couple of weeks. Can't seem to win at anything ... the wife is sick and I took the kid up state to go to college over the weekend. Just give me a couple more days and I will get you the money. Really I can," Tommy begged.

"What you got Tom, a secret stash of money and you hedged your bets with me so you wouldn't have to touch it? You got a CD coming due in the next couple days?" Charlie's voice changed from sarcastic to ice cold. "How are you going to get me $50,000 by Thursday?"

"I can do it Charlie. I've got an inside tip, all I need is $25,000 for the bet and I can pay you off, with interest and have enough left over to start betting again. Please...you've known me since we were kids. You know I'm good for it."

There was silence on the other side of the lights. Tom knew there were lights, because the glare was coming through the blindfold and his face felt like it was getting sunburned. God, it must be some sort of spotlight, just inches from me. Not all the sweating was because of the light.

Tommy prayed that Charlie would take the offer. It was a long shot, but if he bet across the board and the horse ended up in the money, he would be home free. If he lost, he was already packed and ready to skip town.

"Tommy, I believe you, and just for old time's sake I'm considering your offer. You realize I have a business to run and a reputation to keep. If I let you get off without paying, other customers will think I am weak. People won't pay what they owe and the other bookies will try to move in on my territory. You need to put up a little 'good faith' just to keep my reputation intact. You understand … right?"

"Sure, Charlie, I understand, how about I give you my car. It's a classic and worth at least half what I owe … does that make us square for a few days?"

Again, Charlie paused. "I'd like to consider the offer, Tom, but you are tied to a chair and can't get to your pocket … and besides … it doesn't square up the debt. I'm still out $25,000 and you want me to spot you another $25,000. How about another asset Tommy boy, do you have anything else I can use until your horse comes in?"

Tommy sat in the chair, thinking of anything he had that would keep him breathing and in one piece. His shoulders fell, chin lying on his chest. "I got nothing Charlie. I got nothing. I'm at your mercy."

Charlie laughed, "Tommy, you know bookies have no mercy. I think I have an idea. I will give you a challenge. If you make the right decision, I'll extend your payment date for two weeks." He nodded and two of his men released Tommy from the chair, then hung his tied hands over a hook and raised him until he was standing on his toes.

Somebody took the blindfold off. As his eyes adjusted to the dim light of the warehouse, he saw Charlie and his goons.

One of them was standing on a ladder right next to him with a rope in his hand. The creep placed a noose over Tommy's head, and threw the other end of the rope high above, over one of the steel beams in the warehouse ceiling. He climbed down the ladder and secured the loose end to a nearby pole. He gave Tommy a wry smile.

He was scared. *Things couldn't get any worse*, he thought. Then he saw her.

"Oh, God ... no." His wife, held by two of Charlie's goons, was carried to the center of the cavernous room. They tied her hands together and cinched her neck with one end of the rope. They placed her hands over the hook. She was on her toes. Her eyes were as big as dinner plates. Gagged, she tried to scream at Tommy. No one could understand her muffled tirade, but he could see the hatred in her eyes.

"Charlie you can't do this. Betty is innocent. She didn't place the bets, I did. You can't punish her for my mistakes!" he pleaded.

Charlie laughed. He seemed to be enjoying Tommy's discomfort. Sitting at a small table, he slowly poured himself a drink. "Ah, single malt ... now that can relax a man and give him time to think."

Charlie sipped his drink in silence. "I have decided to give you a choice, Tommy. Personally, I think this is a fair way for you discover the type of man you are. I'm going to have the two of you raised about two feet off the ground—by your hands. The slack in the rope will be tightened, but not too tight ... we wouldn't want you to slip and snap your neck."

Charlie thought that was funny. He and his men laughed for several seconds.

"George is going to count down from ten. That gives you ten seconds to decide if you want Betty to live—or you. I will tell you," Charlie paused for dramatic effect, "the arms will be dropped slowly, this means it won't break the neck, just cause one of you to slowly strangle to death. I will finish my drink and one of you will pay your debt. If you don't make a decision, I'll hang you both."

"Charlie, that won't solve our problem. If you kill me, you won't get the money and if you kill Betty, my only reason for living ends. I won't be able to function to get you the money."

"True my boy, but if you are dead, I keep face among my other clients and competitors. Let her live and I can find a place for her in the organization. If she dies and you don't get me the money, I can still kill you. No matter what happens, after word gets out about today; I win."

"By the way, don't worry about the car. I'll get your keys when we're finished. Either way, the missus won't need to drive some broken down rattle trap piece of shit that isn't worth the cost of changing the title."

Charlie nodded, George called out … "Ten."

"Betty, I am so sorry this has happened. I just had no control."

"Nine."

"I wish I had a way to make this up to you."

"Eight."

"I wish she could say something. Charlie, please let her talk to me!"

"Seven."

One of the men removed the gag. Betty gasped a solid breath of air and spit at Tommy.

"Six."

"I've got nothing to say to you, you…BASTARD," she screamed. "I've had no use for you for years."

"Five."

"Baby, I'm so sorry. Please forgive me. At least let

me know that I'm forgiven and you still love me."

"Four."

"You want forgiveness, Tommy, see a priest. You want love; visit a whore. I loathe you."

"Three."

Charlie smiled. Looking at both of them, he held out his hands, palms up, and shrugged his sholders.

"Two."

Betty twisted and turned on the rope enough to face Charlie. "For once in your miserable life Tommy— be a man—make the right decision."

"One."

"Hang her...hang her! I want to live. I'll rob a bank for you to get the money, just hang her," Tommy screamed as his body was racked with sobs.

"Zero."

Tommy felt the rope tighten around his neck as his hands lowered. He watched his wife descend towards the ground, unharmed. Her hands were untied and the noose taken from her neck. She casually walked over to Charlie and put her arm around his waist. She kissed him on the lips. Looking Tommy in the eye, she spat, "Surprise loser."

Tommy struggled for air. He was dizzy and things looked fuzzy. He kicked his legs, tried to get his hands up to grab the rope. His body swung freely just inches off the floor. Black spots were starting to block his vision.

"Can you hear me, Tommy…I worked out a deal with Charlie. I paid off your debt with money I stole and hid from you. I'm giving it to Charlie on the condition that you die a slow and painful death." Betty's betrayal was stunning. Tommy continued kicking.

Charlie walked around the table and opened the case. Inside was $50,000 in new twenty dollar bills. "This guarantees your son's education and a proper place in my organization when he graduates from law school, Babe. I have to admit, you are smooth—stealing Tom's money without his noticing and setting up this deal to get rid of him.

"Tommy was an idiot. I have hated him for years," Betty said as she poured herself a drink.

I have given it a lot of thought and I am afraid I couldn't trust you in my organization. How would I know you weren't stealing from me or turn against me with my competitors or the cops? Besides you're too old and worn out to be a serious earner in one of my clubs."

With deceptive quickness, Charlie placed a gun to her head and pulled the trigger. Her brains splattered on Tommy's legs and stomach.

Charlie laughed as he looked up and realized that Tommy, who was still alive, had watched his wife die and knew he was soon to follow.

As the life drained from his body, Tommy quit kicking. He was cut down—his body thudded to the floor, landing next to his wife.

"Get the money and call a clean-up crew. Spread the word to every gambler, bookie, and their families how Tommy's debts were paid. Describe what happened, in detail, and let everyone know that we settle accounts the old fashion way.

"One last thing, find the boy and keep an eye on him. Send a couple of our attorneys to talk with him. We could use a young smart lawyer." Charlie said to no one in particular. He finished his drink in one gulp.

Autumn Leaves

"**I** am damn sick and tired of those leaves," Jeff grumbled looking out the bay window. "I raked the yard not two hours ago and everything is piled up again."

He continued to mutter to himself as he watched the leaves falling from his neighbor's trees. The wind whipped the leaves in a cyclone that seemed to transport every leaf in the neighborhood to his yard. One large swirl flashed by the window. Jeff jumped back as he seemed to be looking into the face of some kind of multi-colored monster smiling at him.

"That's it ... I've had enough," he shouted to the empty room. I've got just the thing for you sons of bitches." His eyes flashed with near madness as he hit the starter on his sixty-two inch riding mower. Attached to the back was the new Turbo Leaf Eater 6000 (TLE 6000), with a thirty-three to one grinder that would pulverize leaves, sticks, branches, or anything else in the yard to near dust. The twin hundred-gallon collection bins would more than take care of his problem.

Jeff laughed as he sat atop the large mower waiting for the garage door to open. He deftly pulled onto the driveway, then attacked the front yard with relish, following his well-established cutting pattern. Pile after pile of leaves disappeared into the hopper as he drove back and forth. The mower cut each swath of grass as it sucked the leaves into the Turbo Leaf Eater where they were pulverized, then deposited into bins for disposal.

He made a second and a third trip around the yard; challenging every leaf in the neighborhood to invade his world. He vowed and cursed the wind as more and more leaves accepted his challenge. They landed in his yard, challenging Jeff and his TLE 6000 to a fight to the death.

Jeff passed over his "oil pit" hidden in the back of his yard. He used the forty-foot deep pit to dispose of old oil and other items that would cost him a fortune to recycle. Both mower bins were full. Jeff laughed as he stopped his mower, and dumped the two bins into the pit. He pulled his Turbo away from the hole and dropped in a lit match.

Flames jumped twenty feet in the air as the dust and oil caught fire. Leaves continued to fall, Jeff shook his fist as he stared up at the trees and shouted, "Eat shit and die, you won't be back to haunt me now."

Again, he fired up the motor. The leaves had to go if he had to stay on the mower all night long. The winds came up. Hard and driving it began to build, small tornados of dried leaves joined together, whipping against his skin, mocking him. They began to cling to his mower and clothing.

Jeff made a pass by the big bay window; his young son was watching the battle. Jeff waved to his son and was surprised when the boy ran screaming from the room.

Turning for another trip around the front yard, the mower seemed to tilt, as though slipping on an embankment. It seemed to lift into the air and the engine whined as no resistance met the powerful blades. Jeff looked around, realizing he and his TLE 6000 were no longer on the ground.

He began to spiral. He was caught in one of the leaf tornados, but he didn't care. Again, he challenged the autumn leaves. "You think this will stop me? I will chase you to the gates of hell and grind you to dust."

Suddenly, the wind howled, "No!" as the face once again appeared in front of Jeff.

"I am Kohana, Goddess of leaves. You shall hurt us no more!" Kohana spread her giant multicolored arms, embraced Jeff, and his mower.

They began to spin, much faster this time. The dry leaves cut into his skin, while the tender leaves caressed him. They attached themselves to his body, becoming a part of him. The mower vanished; Jeff no longer heard or felt the vibration of the machine beneath him.

Kohana gripped him. He felt as light as the air all around him. He began to see the beauty of the autumn leaves. He was no longer separated from the leaves. It was as if he and the leaves had become one. He wondered why he had been so angry.

He flew with the leaves, into yards up and down his street. He was lifted to great heights, traveling far beyond the trees that had released them.

Jeff swirled past his house one last time, past the bay window. His son and wife stood looking into the yard. He tried to wave, but he was no longer human; he had become a part of the swirling mass of autumn color that whipped past the window.

For a second time, the boy jumped back from the window and hugged his mother's legs. Andrea, the boy's mother asked, "What's the matter son, you seem frightened?" Shaking, he pointed to the swirling mass of leaves and said "Daddy."

If I Had Known

If I had only known the price I would pay for answering the phone, I would have let it ring. It was in the middle of the night, and I never get calls past ten. I knew it had to be bad news, someone had died … or worse.

I answered on the fifth ring. If my answering machine had been working, I could have just listened to the message. *This had better be good, calling at this hour of the night.* I thought to myself.

"Andy … Andy, its Donna, please don't hang up. I'm in trouble. People are trying to kill me. I'm in a warehouse on South Tenth. God … I'm scared. Please come get me."

"Lady, you got the wrong number. Try again." I shouted and slammed the phone into its cradle.

Less than a minute later, the phone rang again.

"What!"

"Andy, help me … you have to help me. Carlos is after me. Says he is going to auction me to the highest bidder because you took his product and owe him money. You've got to help."

"Lady, you got the wrong number and the wrong man. Like I said the last time, there is nobody here named "Andy." Ask Carlos if he will forget about you if you tell him where this Andy is. Who knows, he might show you mercy. And get your story straight, is he going to kill you or sell you?"

"Whoever you are, please help me. I can make it worth your while...I can."

Curiosity kicked in. I was broke and out of a job, the thought of some pocket money put a whole new spin on this gig. I talked to the woman.

"Larry, my name is Larry. I doubt there is anything you could give me to make it worth putting my ass on the line against this Carlos and his people; especially at three in the morning, but make me an offer."

"Look, Larry. I'm in warehouse fifteen on South Tenth Street. Carlos is searching number three, so there is still time to come and get me. I'll be in the back of the warehouse, hidden at the rear door, surrounded by boxes. Come get me. Please. I'll give you $5,000."

I really wondered what was going on. If the woman was several buildings from the gang, why hadn't she made a run for it while they were searching the other warehouses? Then again, five grand is more money than I've seen in a long time.

"All right I'll come, but listen, I don't have a car, I ride a Harley; those guys will hear me coming. When you hear the bike, be ready. We'll be out of there before they know what's going on. See you in twenty minutes."

I dressed quickly, all black, all leather; grabbed my Glock, checked the magazine and hit the door. I turned onto the highway at seventy miles per hour and headed south towards the warehouse district.

At Tenth Street, I turned as quietly as a Harley will allow. I let it idle along in second gear. With highway sounds echoing off the building, I hoped I wouldn't be seen or heard.

I could see several buildings along the fence. Four men stepped out of nowhere, from between two warehouses and blocked my path. I was at building eight. The Harley coasted to a stop about fifteen feet from the four guys. Crossing my arms, I held the butt of my gun under my jacket. "May I help you, gentlemen?" I asked rather condescending.

"We're looking for someone, why are you here so early in the morning?" the leader asked.

"I'm moving here. I'm building a clubhouse down a bit farther and I'm living in it. Now, get out of the way."

Mr. I'm-In-Charge laughed, "Not likely, my boss owns these buildings." He started to raise his shotgun. My hand left my jacket and four shots later, I was racing to the warehouse.

I pulled around back of warehouse fifteen just as Donna came out from behind the boxes stacked against the back wall. She wore a light coat and carried a large courier bag across her shoulder. Without a word, she climbed on the back of the bike.

I coasted the big Harley forward. This time, I headed down the side of the far buildings. I realized why she had not tried to escape, no back gate.

"I heard shots," Donna yelled into my ear.

I nodded but remained focused on the spaces between the buildings. No one tried to stop us. I left the warehouse strip and headed for the blacktop. As I dropped it into fifth gear, I let the Harley run—full open. We wrapped around the interstate.

Miles later, I slowed and said in her ear, "No one is following, where can I take you?"

"I don't know. I can't go home, they will be waiting. Andy's place is just as dangerous. I have nowhere to go. Take me to the bus station. I can catch the next bus to anywhere."

"Turn your phone off so you can't be tracked. There are no buses this time of the morning. How big a deal is this Carlos dude?"

"He runs drugs, girls, and launders money. He has a lot of guys working for him, very bad guys."

"Okay, here's what we're going to do. We'll get a bite to eat and sit tight for a few hours. Then I'll fill my tank and get you away from the city. You can catch a bus or train and get away, far away. You can start over; go to a place where they won't be looking for you."

I headed to IHOP. The coffee is strong and the food is hot. Around dawn, we got back on the bike and headed for gas and a quick route out of town.

A truck stop provided the perfect place to gas up. I grabbed a few snacks and bottles of water and checked the state wall map for a safe route out of harm's way.

"We'll head west on the two lane. By not taking the interstate, it will take us a little longer, but we can travel unseen. I thought caution was the best action, especially if this Carlos had a wide network of people.

I checked the parking lot one last time then hit the highway, traveling the speed limit; time seemed to stand still as the miles rolled by. I kept one eye on the rear view, just in case. We passed through dozens of small towns and a hundred miles later, I was looking for a bus stop.

Another thirty miles brought me to a medium sized town, with a Greyhound bus station and a built in eatery. After a cup of coffee, I said, "Here you go. Get a bus ticket to anywhere and a start fresh."

"How can I thank you, or ever repay you?" She asked as she handed me the money.

"Simple, don't ever call me again."

I fired up the Harley and headed back towards home—sticking to the back roads. I wasn't worried about being seen—the sun was rising, and the scenery made the trip worthwhile.

I was about fifty miles from home when a white Caddie pulled in front of me and stopped. I hit the brakes and fishtailed, as my front tire touched the front passenger door on the Cadillac. I was looking into the double barrels of a sawed off shotgun. "Damn." I killed the Harley and slowly took off my helmet.

"Gentlemen, I have insurance, no need to get this upset over a little accident." My mind raced to find a way to escape or grab my gun before he could pull the trigger.

"Keep your hands on the handlebars and your mouth shut, asshole. We're waiting for someone."

Timed crawled, I had to find a way out of this mess. It took twenty minutes before a black Caddie pulled up behind, bumping my rear fender.

I turned to see Mr. I'm-In Charge, or whatever his name was, climb out of the back seat; his arm in a sling. *Guess I didn't finish the job at the warehouse, too bad for me.*

Exiting from the other rear door was a mountain of a man dragging Donna. "Mountain" tossed her to the ground near my feet. A third man exited the driver's side.

"Hola' asshole. We haven't been properly introduced; I'm Carlos. You would have gotten away, but the bitch had her phone on."

If looks could have killed, I would have turned her into rotting meat at that very instant.

"We tracked you from the interstate and set the trap while you were in town. Ricardo took the back road. I watched the interstate until you headed out. Now, get off the bike."

I put down the kickstand, stood, and turned towards Carlos. What would happen would happen, and Carlos would give the order.

Donna stared up at me, eyes full of fear.

"You should have turned off your phone." I said.

Carlos smiled as he stared at her. "You are a lot of trouble, girl. We found Andy; he said you took the money and the product." Looking at me, he asked her, "How did you get asshole here to help you?"

Not waiting for an answer, Carlos motioned with his head, and Mountain put a bullet in the back of Donna's neck. Coming out, the bullet removed the front of her throat, lower jaw and her right ear. She was dead the moment the bullet severed her spine.

"I could have taken her back to town and let her pay for her sins," Carlos explained, "but she needed to set an example for anyone else thinking they could cross me."

Carlos looked through me. "Okay asshole, I'm not interested in how or why you got involved. Let me say that *this*," pointing towards Donna's dead, mutilated body, "took something from me. It was returned when we picked her up. *This* has been punished. Now what do I do with you?"

I stood, waiting for the nod of his head and blackness to devour my brain. I waited.

Carlos seemed to have made his decision. "Tell you what, gringo; I'm going to give you a choice," he said making a gun with his fingers and pointing it to my head. "I could end your miserable life quick and painless; after all, you simply got sucked into this little party. I could let you live after my boys break every bone in your body and you figure a way to get to a hospital from here, which means you would probably die a slow and painful death. Or you can ride free, provided you and your bike make deliveries for me."

It was a tough choice; yeah right. I did have the nerve to ask how many deliveries before my debt was paid. Carlos laughed.

Yes sir, if I had known the price, I would have never answered the phone. My life of slavery started with a $5,000 down payment but the good news is—I have a steady paycheck with extra benefits.

The bad news? There is no retirement, and the career path can be cut short on a moment's notice.

Castle of Night

Sometimes glamour is not what it seems.

William checked his appearance one last time then looked out the window at the arriving guests. He remembered the night he arrived at the ball ...

The invitation was engraved with gold plate, and delivered by a private messenger who said he would return within the hour. Just holding the envelope seemed to suck the life out of him. He sat down, broke open the seal, and read the note:

> *Sir William,*
>
> *You are invited to the annual All Hallows Eve Ball held at the fortress of Princess Selene of the Woodlands.*
>
> *With the rising of the sun,*
> *Lives will be changed forever.*

Attached was a second note of instruction. The ball requires that all guests dress as the person they wish to become, or represent an ancestor of great achievement. Only six items may be added to the costume for personal use, come alone and do not mention the invitation to anyone.

Keeping this secret until after the ball was no problem. William's young wife was away visiting family. By the time she returned, the ball would be over and their lives changed.

William's thoughts returned to the ball. He had heard stories at court; whispers in hallways, or short conversations heard behind doorways. Nothing one could count on. Yet the stories and the strange happenings persisted.

Talk of families disappearing, rumors of enslavement to the Woodlands family, human sacrifice, and other things so terrible they simply could not be repeated.

There were also tales of great debauchery at the ball. On the night of the ball, no one at the castle was bound by any rules—much less remorse.

It was said that each person lived his or her darkest and wildest fantasies. Many discovered what kind of person they really were when unfettered by society's norms or morality.

Some said that those who disappeared were given great lands and wealth in in faraway places. Fortune and power was the desire of all who accepted.

William jumped at the knock at his door. The messenger did not linger for permission but quietly entered, bowed, and waited for the answer. William looked directly into the man's eyes and said, "Yes." The messenger placed an envelope on the table and left the room.

William quickly opened the missive, careful not to tear the parchment. A carriage would arrive at dusk on All Hallows Eve. William had ninety seconds to enter the carriage or use the time as his final opportunity to change his mind.

William spent two days considering his life, his position, and power that attending the ball could bring him. He poured himself another cognac, each time returning to his chair to work out his answer. His wealth and power were growing, but not as fast as he had hoped. His political career was on the rise and with time, he would be a member of the King's court with his lovely wife by his side. His young son would have great opportunities never before afforded to his family. Opportunities that could take years of hard work and political maneuvering—with no guarantee of success.

The day of the ball arrived. William, still torn between doing something he might regret for the rest of his life, and securing a place in society for himself and his young family, was finally convinced that he must accept the invitation. He had only the remaining hours of the afternoon to select his costume.

William chose to look into his past for a suitable costume; he wanted to be different, to be noticed by the Princess Selene. He found many officer's uniforms in a long forgotten room of the house. They had belonged to generations of Highlanders. He chose a formal dress uniform and a cloak. No armor. The uniform would keep him warm and the hidden pouches and pockets might prove to be useful. He selected five of his six objects, each of which would remain unseen. Strapping his sword to his side, he was ready.

When the carriage arrived, he was waiting at the bottom of the steps. He entered the carriage with a calm confidence that he hoped impressed the driver. William strained to see the driver's face, but he wore a hooded cloak.

Curtains drawn, the six large stallions pulled the carriage with frightening speed toward its destination. The driver was powerful and large enough to control the horses without incident.

William sat in the speeding carriage, still and tense, bracing himself against the sway of the carriage and preparing for what lay ahead. He pulled back the carriage curtains but found that the windows had been blackened.

The driver coaxed the nervous horses around the circular driveway, stopping in front of the massive, wooden door of Woodland Castle. William straightened himself as he exited the coach and marched up the stairs.

The castle's brightly lit turrets, barely kept the darkness at bay. The backlit stained glass window cast an ominous glow. There were six carriages waiting to disgorge their single occupants. Once empty, they vanished into the night.

He presented himself to the court herald ... "William of the Highlands, Son of Eric the Red, Grandson of Fizer, ruler of the Emerald Mountains.," The princes stood a few feet from the herald.

William knelt on one knee before the Princess; his sheathed sword held in his outstretched hands. He looked up into the face of the most beautiful woman he had ever seen. Her eyes a deep ocean blue. William felt he could lose himself in those eyes, perhaps for a lifetime.

"My lady," William stammered, "I present you with one of my six personal items as a sign of my loyalty to you and your family. I request its return only to do your bidding."

"An interesting entrance Sir William of the Highlands, mingle with the others; enjoy yourself with slave, staff, and guest. Prove yourself worthy to join my court."

Dismissed, William walked the long hall, towards the sound of music and voices. He heard several announcements as the other guests arrived. Each guest presented with great flair and authority. For the first time he began to wonder what chance he had to win the right for great riches and power.

Two servants welcomed him into the great hall. William entered on to a balcony. He stopped to look at the sea of guests below him. His heart sank as he saw the wealth of those attending the ball. The quality of their clothing and the value of their jewelry made him wish he had dressed up instead of down for the occasion.

The second thing he realized was that even if each invited guest had come alone; they now had at least one escort on their arm. It was obvious that the stories of debauchery were true.

Along the walls, people were in various stages of undress performing disturbing acts as others gorged themselves at the long table packed with food. The servants of the princess wore only thin sheets of cloth, which slipped over their heads and then loosely knotted at the waist with a gold cord to allow easy access to their bodies. The guests—bleary eyed with lust, exploited this accessibility, disrobing the servants at will.

Lost in thought, he jerked back to reality when he heard his name. Turning his head, a young female with blond hair falling below her waist bowed to him.

"I am Elizabeth, your escort for the ball." Her voice flowed over his body. He felt his will slipping away. His mind, as well as his body excited.

He felt warm and his manhood grew as he continued to stare at her. Her skin was alabaster white and looked as soft as new fallen snow; her eyes were the same ocean blue as the princess. They seemed to draw William to her. Without speaking, she called to him with promises of pleasure beyond his imagination. He suddenly felt her need. She desired him and promised excitement that no woman had ever offered him.

Although gentle by nature, he fantasized slapping her, pulling her hair, forcing her to kneel before him and prepare for another blow. He wanted to rip her gown and take her hard, dry, and violent.

She smiled, sensing his passion; as she slowly played with the knot that held her dress closed. "I am here to serve and fulfill all your wishes and desires." She whispered, opening her gown. She invited William to feast upon her flesh.

Somehow, William gained control of himself, he didn't know how until he felt warmth from one of his pockets. The "Orb of Right" handed down from father to son for generations that dated back to his Celtic ancestors. The Orb had returned him to himself.

William smiled at the woman, but did not look into her eyes. *I must not look into the eyes of the servants.* He knew that the stories of debauchery were true, the weakness of the guests and bewitching powers of the servants dismantled the decency of those attending the ball.

The servants encouraged their charges to perform acts found in the darkest recesses of their minds—hidden things. Unthinkable fantasies emerged as the darkness grew in their minds, consuming them.

William followed the woman down the staircase and into the great hall. He made his way to the table of food, and quietly nibbled on bits of meat and fruit as he observed those around him.

He studied the activities of the other guests and staff, and could not understand why a woman would allow herself to be chained to a wall and whipped while other guests abused her body. The woman moaned in pleasure as various guests hit, bit, and prodded her.

William attempted to take leave of his escort. She moved closer to him, caressing him, luring him with her scent and her promises to meet his deepest fantasy to possess her, own her, and in the name of pleasure do the cruelest things to her.

"Allow me to finish eating in peace. Perhaps you can go get us something strong to drink. I will need it to strengthen me for what we are about to do." He touched her cheek with the back of his hand then slowly raked his fingernails down to her chin. He hoped that this act would convince her that he planned to fall into her trap.

Elizabeth smiled. "Yes my lord" she whispered. William, looking at her mouth and not her eyes, noticed the fangs, protruding ever so slightly from under her top lip.

Vampire, he thought. *They must all be vampires and tonight we are their special feast.*

He knew he had to get out of the ballroom and find a way to stop them before the hundred or so people became the celebration meal for these creatures of hell.

William had noticed the servants entering and exiting the hall behind tapestry that hid archways and open passages. He made his way to the tapestry, and found one of the hidden openings. Just as Elizabeth returned to the banquet table with their drinks, he managed to slip out of sight. He knew she would find him. He must find a way out of the castle.

Torches burned in carriers attached the walls of the long hallway. William could hear the voices of the servants as he hid in the shadows. When he found a door, he listened but heard nothing.

Entering quietly, he searched for his escape. *I must find the right path through the maze. It will lead me to the back entrance,* he thought to himself as he frantically looked for a way out. If he stayed, he would be forced to fight—he wouldn't have a chance without the sword of his ancestors. He did have his hidden weapons. The Orb of Right would keep him from falling under the control of the monsters in the castle.

The only exit from the room was the way he had entered. Once again, William listened carefully before opening the door and slipping into the hallway. His cloak was dark and helped disguise his presence among the shadows. He kept his hands on his remaining weapons.

Three steps down the hall and a lilting voice froze him in his tracks. "William, you are so bad, leaving the party unattended. Now I'm afraid you must be punished." Elizabeth's soft voice whispered in his ear. William slowly turned to discover that the lovely vampire, fangs fully extended had plans of her own. She also had one of the large male servants with her. His face seemed to form the snout of an animal, while hair sprouted all over his body.

The Lycan growled, " … come with me human." He licked his lips and placed his hand on Williams shoulder. Without hesitation, William's right hand came out from under the cloak, the silver blade pushed into the werewolf's throat. Its eyes went wide in surprise then blank.

William turned to Elizabeth; his left hand thrust forward and pushed the thin wooden stake into her heart. Elizabeth stared in disbelief then turned to dust.

He ran down the hall, wanting to get away from the body on the floor and the possibility of being seen by other servants or guards. Despite all his years of training in fighting and weapons, William knew he had been lucky. He was vastly outnumbered and he was the only human willing to stand against these evil creatures. Luck would not keep him safe much longer.

At last, William saw lights at the end of the hall. Soon he would be out of the castle and on his way home. He passed through the tapestry and found himself back into the main ballroom. Bloodlust filled the air.

Werewolves and vampires were fighting over the dead and dying bodies of the guests. The princess stood on her throne while her vampire servants fought to protect her. She looked at William. "Help me ... be my champion and defeat these creatures," she cried as she tossed his sword to him.

William became a man possessed, using both sword and sheath; he showed no mercy for werewolf, vampire, or human. All died. Most guests were already dead and he soullessly dispatched the dying. Humans were ripped to shreds by the beasts he now had the pleasure of destroying.

William no longer heard the growls of the werewolves or the shrieks of the vampires. Movement meant monster, and monster meant death. It was his life in exchange for their death. He could not stop killing until all movement ceased.

Exhausted, he gained control of himself. Realizing he was the only living creature in the room, he began to relax. He had won.

Remaining cautious, William stood in the middle of the ballroom, keeping close watch on the bodies to ensure nothing would attack him from one of the hidden archways.

He did search for someone. The one person he knew he had not killed. At last, he heard a small laugh coming from the throne. The princess sat without fear. Smiling down at him, she applauded his accomplishment.

"You Sir William of the Highlands are my champion. For the first time in over two-hundred years, someone has met the challenge. Now your life will be changed forever." Her voice echoed in his head. Her fangs flashed as she laughed.

William reached one last time into his cloak and tossed the flask filled with holy water at the creature. It represented the power of a new religion. The parishioners placed great faith in its power. The flask fell on the feet of the princess. She laughed as the water splashed on her.

"I'm far too old for this foolish young religion to affect me." She growled and raised her arms. As she spoke, the vampires reappeared as smoke rose from the floor. They stood quietly, facing their mistress. "You will now call me Mistress Selene."

No words were spoken, yet the vampires turned and charged William in mass. They were fast and efficient as they dragged him before the princess and pulled his head to the side. The princess leaned down and smiled, "Welcome to the family." William's world went black.

He awoke, chained to a wall. He hungered, he craved something and yet, he didn't know what or why. He had blacked out, but it couldn't have been more than a few hours. The door opened, two young werewolves and three female vampires entered.

"Ah...tonight is your lucky night, cousin," Growled the larger of the two half-men. "There are gifts awaiting you in the ballroom." They smiled and the vampires giggled. William worried about what was now in store, yet he felt consumed by unknown hungers, they overwhelmed his ability to think.

His escorts led him up from the depths of the castle to the ballroom. The princess remained on her throne, dressed in the same gown, beautiful as ever. William was drawn to her, unable to escape her stare.

"Sir William, a year has passed; you have survived the time of fasting. It is now time for your final initiation into the family." She announced to those in the hall.

William stood in shock. It could not have been a year; he was only unconscious for a short time—outside it was still dark.

He looked around and stared at all the bodies. They were tonight's guests. They had failed to pass the test and were ripped apart and drained of blood, flesh and bone.

Movement from behind Saline's tapestries caught William's eye. He felt weak and devastated when his wife and son were dragged between him and the princess.

William dropped to his knees as the werewolves released him. He knew why families disappeared. There was no new world, no great riches and no power or entry into the kings' court. There was only a future of death and blood.

"Feed William, fulfill your destiny. Be the last of your line, and ... live forever," she commanded.

William lunged at his son. He heard his wife scream as he plunged his fangs in the child's throat. Felt him struggle, and then slowly become still as his life's blood was taken from him—one gulp at a time.

William stood and looked at his wife. He saw her tears, heard her sobs and last words... "I love you"...as he ripped her dress and threw her to the floor. She was face down when he mounted her, pulled her head back, and ripped out her throat. He fed the two unquenchable hungers that possessed him. Finished, he rose and bowed to the princess.

"Sir William of the Highlands, at your service, my lady," he said with a smile, fangs fully extended...

It was dusk. For the past six- hundred years, the guests had arrived, the limos lining the drive. They always dressed to impress, believing their lives would be changed forever—and so they would.

There had been no one worthy of joining the family since he survived so many years ago.

William bowed his head and remembered.

Sometimes glamour ...

Knock, Knock

Three Knocks, then three more—that is how it started.

J anice, awakened by the knock, shook Stephen's shoulder. "Stephen, someone's knocking on the door. Who is it? What's wrong?" Jolted awake as she shook him, he was instantly aware of her fear.

Stephen ran down the stairs, and switched on the front door security camera. "Thomas. It is three in the morning. Go Home."

"How'd you know it was me?" the voice from the speaker slurred, "Oh Yeah, the camera. Open up, I need to talk to the two of you."

"Go Home Thomas, sleep it off. We can talk tomorrow over several cups of strong coffee."

Stephen hadn't made it up four steps when the drunk on the other side of the door began pounding. As Stephen continued to climb the stairs to his bedroom, the pounding went from three pounds and a pause to four … then five … and finally a constant pounding.

Janice met him on the stairs. "What is happening?" she demanded as she stared at the door, expecting the solid steel barrier to buckle from abuse.

"It's Tom, drunk, belligerent, and it sounds like he is looking for a fight. He will wear himself out in a bit and go home."

Janice shot down the steps two at a time. Punching the speaker button, she yelled. "Tommy, get the hell out of here or I'm calling the cops. It's Friday night, I will press charges and you can spend the weekend in lock up."

"Open the door, Bitch. You won't call the cops or anyone else. I know the secret. I'll spill the beans and you and that shit of a new husband will lose everything." He began laughing hysterically. "The house, cars, bank accounts—they will all be mine if you don't let me in." He resumed beating on the door.

Stephen shook his head, went to the closet and pulled out a pair of cotton robes. Janice's husband considered the entire house a playroom for the two of them. Janice laughed when he had hung the full-length robes in the closet for their protection in case company dropped by while they were romping downstairs naked.

"Open the door you bastards. I know you're standing there. I don't hear sirens you cowardly shits. Open up, it's time to face the music!"

Janice and Stephen locked eyes as Stephen opened the door. Standing side by side, they stared at Thomas. His left hand was wrapped in a bandage; the other was bloody from beating on the door. He was drunk, dirty, and filled with anger.

Thomas started to charge through the door but Stephens fist connected with his stomach. Thomas stopped in his tracks and doubled over. He let out a gasp but didn't vomit. Janice assumed he had already thrown up before he arrived at the house. Slowly he rose; most of the fight taken out of him.

"Okay dickhead. You are welcome to enter our home, provided you remain civil and a gentleman." Stephen looked at the beaten man. He knew he could escalate into an angry lunatic in seconds, but for now, he was quiet.

As Thomas walked through the front door, Stephen pointed down the hall. "You know where the bathroom is. Go shower. I will give you a change of clothes. You aren't going to ruin my furniture by sitting on it."

Thomas shuffled down the hall. Janice went to make coffee. Thirty minutes later, Thomas entered the living room, cowed, and ashamed of his actions. He collapsed on the couch. Taking a cup of coffee to his lips with a shaking hand, he looked across the coffee table at the *newlyweds*.

After a few moment of silence he stared at Stephen, and said, "I over stepped my bounds tonight, I apologize. But I know what's going on, I know what you did and I'm here to get her back."

Janice stared at him confused, but said nothing. Stephen on the other hand, snickered. "Okay, buddy. Tell me all about your eye opening revelation."

Thomas reached across the table and poured a second cup from the silver server, his hand more steady. For dramatic effect, he leaned back on the couch and took a sip. As the cup lowered, he had a small smile that didn't quite reach his eyes.

Thomas held up his bandaged hand. "I got injured at work today, electrical shock; working on a copy machine. It knocked me all the way across the room, and I must have blacked out for a couple minutes. When I woke up, I started having flashbacks—memories. Things I knew couldn't have happened and yet, I knew that they did. Let me tell you a story ..."

Thomas continued, "A year ago Janice and I were married. We were happy; I had a great job with the largest bank in the country. We were making plans for our future. Steve, you were my best friend. You were always spending time at our house, the three of us going places and doing things. It never seemed out of place."

Thomas seemed to pause as he considered Steve's constant involvement in their lives. "Three months ago, I woke up, single. I couldn't remember ever being married, but when I would see you, Janice I knew we had some sort of a connection. I knew I worked at the research facility repairing machinery, but I had no memory of any friends, family or social life. I simply went home at night and watched television. I never gave it a thought."

"After the accident this morning, I remembered my life had been different. It seemed strange, one day I'm a bank executive the next I'm working a dead end job. I've lost my wife, my home, everything.

"Steve and I were no longer best friends, hell we aren't even associates. We crossed paths at work, but he's a big shot research scientist and I don't even rate a greeting from him in the mornings.

I would see him watching me as I worked in various departments and it was like he was keeping tabs on me, but I couldn't figure out why."

Glaring at Stephen he continued, "I knew something was missing, but I couldn't figure it out. Then I got shocked and it all came back. You used drugs and mind control to change my memories, you bastard. You did the same to Janice and you took her, mind, body, and soul. You are going to give me back my life or I'm going ruin yours. I'll do whatever is necessary to get Janice back and put you in your place, Steve."

Janice, shocked, stared opened mouth. Stephen laughed like a man possessed. Tom sat silently, deciding what to do next.

Stephen stiffened, regaining his composure; he removed a remote control from his housecoat pocket.

"Close but no cigar, Tommy-boy. I guess you have earned a full explanation." He hit a button. Janice fell asleep in the chair. "It wasn't drugs or mind control," Stephen continued. "It was a simple change in programming."

Tom started to rise. Stephen pointed the controller at his head, "Sit and get the rest of the story, dip shit, or everything goes black, permanently."

Stephen sat down, but continued to lean forward. He looked like a cat ready to pounce on an unsuspecting mouse.

"No drugs, no mind control, simply programming. You, my old friend, are a top of the line first generation experimental android. For the record, Janice is second generation. Initially, I put the two of you together, created memories and let you 'play house' so I could watch you develop emotions and grow. You two did well; somehow, your circuits eliminated all concepts of your mechanical creation. You became 'human', but something happened I didn't expect.

"My program adjustments for Janice made her the perfect woman, at least for me. After watching the two of you interact, I made some adjustments to both your circuits, provided memories of marriage problems and a divorce for Janice and made you a loser with no memory of the marriage."

Stephen smiled, "You both exceeded my expectations. I shut you both down and upgraded the programing. After the re-boot, I fixed you up with the job at the research center, you became a repair person and Janice became my wife. You were right. The reason you now work at the research center is because no one knew you and to everyone there, you are invisible."

Steven sat back in his chair and continued. "I kept you around because I really like you Tom. You were my first experiment and you are special to me, besides, I wanted to see how your core would process the changes in your programming. If you reverted to your old life, I would then have to eliminate you. "

Steven smiled, "Electrical shock brought back your old life memories. You associated them in ways that made sense to you—drugs and mind control. Now that you know what really happened, I guess you will be nothing but a memory; a small blip in the circuitry known as Janice and as far as the world is concerned, you will be another loser technician who left town."

With that, Stephen pushed the button just as Thomas attempted to rise from the couch but instead collapsed on the floor. Stephen took a small screwdriver, opened the back of Tom's head, and removed two printed circuit boards. He then carried him to the basement to be disposed of later.

He opened a small door on the back of Janice's head and attached two small wires. With his 'droid' controller, he typed in some code, closed the door and carried her to bed.

The next morning, Janice greeted Stephen with a warm kiss. "How did you get rid of Tommy last night?" she asked.

Stephen hugged his wife close to him. "He passed out on the couch, after he calmed down. I let him sleep. You fell asleep in the chair while we were talking so I carried you to bed."

Stephen rolled on top of Janice. Her passion was instantaneous, physical and vocal, as programed. After a shower and dressing, the couple went down stairs.

The couch was empty with the blanket neatly folded and a note stating, 'I'm sorry. I won't bother you again.'

He considered the note to be a bit too much, but Janice was a romantic and he knew she wouldn't give last night another thought. Stephen hugged her and headed for the kitchen to pour some coffee.

Stephen called the lab to tell them that he had several large cases to be picked up at his home and delivered to his research area. Good old Tom … gone and soon forgotten.

His next step would be to install a completely new brain and face before introducing Tom as his new research assistant. Tom will work closely with his assistant Amanda. They will be equals and if things go well, Tom and Amanda will 'run off' to get married. Stephen planned to mold Tom and Amanda's minds into a new Artificial Intelligence unit he was developing.

Combining human and artificial beings opened the door to many possibilities—money, pleasure, and power. Pleasures he had never considered until now. Who knows, the new Tom and Amanda just might join the family.

Eavesdropper

It was a slow Friday for Tim. All the salespeople were out of the office. The few accounts that had responded to the telemarketers had been posted. Tim had nothing to do. Even the paper clip tray had been sorted and he was having trouble staying awake.

He decided to kill some time by walking down to the cafeteria for a soft drink. Tim relished his cubicle walls. He wasn't much for office gossip, and didn't talk much to his co-workers. When he was working, he didn't want to be disturbed as he entered the orders and sales figures into the computer.

But today felt different. He was restless, Even casual, meaningless small talk would be welcomed today.

As he neared the end of the aisle, Coke® in hand, he heard the voices of Bill Watkins and Gerald Daniels. The men's voices carried—their whispers flowing over the fabric wall. The urgency of the whispers caught his attention. He stopped and listened.

"Okay Bill, I've talked with Kenny and he is going to alert me when Janice leaves her office with the deposit. I'll tie up the elevator then ride down with her while you take the stairs to the lower level of the parking garage. Kenny has already flattened her tire. I parked my car near Janice's this morning so it will seem natural for me to walk out with her."

Gerald continued explaining the plan, "When we get near her car and see the flat, I'll call you over and we'll volunteer to change the tire. After the car is jacked up, Kenny will walk over to see what's going on and distract Janice. He'll fake a call to the security office on his two-way. When Janice turns back to us, we will all watch her do the 'funky chicken' when he zaps her with 50,000 volts of electricity. Kenny and I will put her in the car and refill the tire with Fix-a-Flat."

Gerald laughed as he continued, "We'll take her to the old cabin at the lake, have some fun with her and split the cash from the bank deposit. If Janice is worth it, we'll keep her for a while, if not, she can swim with the fishes as soon as we're finished with her."

Tim could almost see Bill nodding his head. He knew Janice parked on one of the underground levels. It was a perk for privacy and staying out of the bad weather. Everyone knew that half the outside salespeople didn't come to work on Friday. There were plenty of empty parking spots ... and the plan sounded credible if properly executed.

Tim walked back the way he had come, turned and headed towards the elevator, talking to himself so the two would know he was he passing by. In the cafeteria, Tim considered what he had heard. He was sorry that he decided to leave the safety of his cubical only to overhear the murderous plan.

He reviewed his choices again, and again. He could do say and do nothing and see if Janice showed up for work on Monday. He could warn her and if nothing happened, he would be accused of spreading a terrorist plot and find himself in trouble with the company, his co-workers, and Janice—maybe the police.

He couldn't tell security; Kenny was the head of security. He considered telling Bill and Gerald he had overheard their plot. They could deny everything by saying they planned a robbery every week as a fantasy, or find a way for Tim to face the charges. His last and best option was to tell them he knew their plan, and wanted in.

Tim admitted he was no criminal, but he read mysteries. Bank Robberies, car thefts, serial killers, anything that provided excitement to his otherwise dull life. From television, movies and books, he knew the mistakes people made when committing a crime, and he just might be helpful in this heist.

The weekly cash deposits were in the tens of thousands of dollars. It was a vending business and the money was always in cash, mostly dollar bills—but who really cares. Dollars are hard to trace. With machines all over the region, cash was collected every Thursday, counted on Friday, and deposited late in the afternoon. Vending machines were the most profitable division in the company. Janice was a beautiful woman. Tim had an idea what kind of 'fun' they had planned for her. Tim had been watching her since the day she started work. Thoughts of Janice helped him relax and sleep at night.

He was about to return to his desk when Bill and Gerald walked in and headed straight to his table. "Hey buddy," said Bill, "got a minute?"

Tim nodded and the two sat down at the table, one on either side. "Look, we know you heard our conversation a little while ago. You forgot I have that security mirror in the corner of my workspace so people can't sneak up on me. I know you are a stand-up guy, so we have a deal for you."

Gerald picked up the conversation, "We decided we need another guy for this to go right. Kenny can't leave the property until later in the afternoon. I'm going to drive Janice's car, Bill will drive his; I need someone to drive my car to the cabin. I'll guarantee you twenty five thousand dollars and all the time with Janice you want."

Tim looked from one to the other, opened mouthed, but no sound came out. Bill continued, "Look, we talked about it and this is perfect. You walk to work, so no one will remember you leaving work. You are the invisible man. I'll give you my ID card to get out the gate. When they investigate, your name won't even be mentioned because you will have never gone to the garage.

"Follow us up to the lake and we can all have some fun and get rich. Tim, this is a good plan, we know things about Janice and she isn't the innocent student she pretends to be. When she comes up missing, her past will surface. Everyone will be looking for her. Just make sure you come to work on Monday. What do you say?"

This had not been one of the options Tim had considered. The guys wanted him to join them. That meant he was worry free and would have enough money to pay off his bills and put some money in the bank. Tim smiled and said, "I'm in."

The plan remained the same, except that five minutes after Bill headed for the elevator, Tim would take the stairs. There were no cameras, no security and he wouldn't be missed.

At 2:30 p.m., Gerald was already in the parking lot; Bill was waiting for the elevator carrying Janice. When the door closed, Tim headed for the exit to the stairway.

Tim tingled with excitement. This was his first criminal act and he was so excited he could hardly contain himself. He decided that all those years of reading mysteries was about to pay off.

His glimpse of Janice told him he had made the right decision. Her long blond hair, short black skirt, and lace blouse excited him. He squinted to get a better look of what she displayed under her blouse.

He reached the parking level just ahead of Kenny; they exchanged a pregnant glance, and Tim walked a bit slower so he would be in place when everything 'went down'.

He walked up to the four of them just as Bill was opening the trunk to get the spare tire. "Need some help?" Tim asked.

"No worries, Tim, I have it under control," Gerald said as Tim received the 50,000 volts on the side of the neck.

It was several hours to the lake and every time Tim began to regain consciousness, Janice would give him another shot of electricity. He heard her say how much fun it was to 'juice' him on different parts of his body.

It was well after dark when Tim finely came around. He was naked, cold, and tied to a table. In the semi-darkness of a battery-operated lamp, he could hear the sounds of three people—no four people talking. He turned his head and moaned, "I should never have trusted them."

Tim never gave a thought as to what was going to happen to him, he already realized he wasn't going to get any money, and if he said anything, the three men would put the blame on him. He assumed he was in for a beating and a warning that if he ever said anything, he would join Janice in the lake.

For hours, he listened as the others satisfied their animal hungers. There were screams, demands and grunts ... all the sounds large animals make during mating season. He had no way to measure the passage of time. Finally, it was quiet. He fell asleep.

He was startled awake by a slap in the face. "What's the matter lover, feeling left out?" Janice asked. "You idiot, everything was planned to the second until you overheard the plan. They were idiots to discuss it at work.

He was still tied to the table. Janice stood at the head of the table, leaning down over him; she kissed him, full on the mouth, with lots of tongue. She bit his lip then flipped the table up on end without taking a deep breath. He could not believe her strength.

The table edge now rested on the dirt floor. *At least I'm upright, not flat on my back,* he thought as he watched Janice parade in front of him, wrapped only in a towel that didn't quite close. She was looking at him like a prize steak in the butcher shop.

"Take a look at the price of failure, fresh meat," she growled as she pivoted the table at the corner. She marched near the bed and held up the lantern.

The three men were lying in their own blood. It was impossible to identify any of the bodies—they were cut to ribbons. The blood had soaked through the mattress and was dripping onto the dirt floor. Body parts were scattered across the room.

Tim gagged. He had never seen anything so horrifying. He realized that the table was some sort of surgical table, which could be tilted at various angles—the top made of cold stainless steel. Janice was smiling. She licked her lips at the site. "God that was fun; but as they say, the party has just begun." Janice walked towards Tim, her hips swaying. He got an unobstructed view of her body as she dropped the towel. "I understand you weren't that interested in the money. You didn't even bother to ask for more than the $25,000 they offered. It must be me you want. Well, sweetheart, those three were the warm up and you're my main event."

Janice tipped the table back to a level position. She climbed up and straddled Tim, despite death looking him in the eye, could not help himself. Janice had been his fantasy since she had been hired six months ago. He had said to someone, "I'd die for some of that." Now it looked like he was going to get his wish.

Janice did all the things that turn a man on and then she experimented with new ways to keep him in the game. Tim had never experienced such pleasures and realized why the other three men had made so much noise.

After an hour, Tim lay on the table, sweat pooled under his body. He was exhausted from the demands Janice had made of him. She had untied him so he could assume some unusual positions. When they had finished, he was too weak to think about escape.

She allowed him to rest a bit, and to eat cold sandwiches and drink a flat soda. He felt better but knew she was faster and stronger and there would be hell to pay if he tried to escape. *There are some things worse than death,* he thought to himself.

"Here's the deal, Tim, as long as you keep me hot or satisfied; you live. If you are good enough to meet my every need and keep up with me until dawn, we can split the $500,000 and go our separate ways. If you fail, I will skin you alive ... and believe me you will still be alive at the end of that party. After I skin you, I will show you such pain you will beg me to end your agony. Oh ... there's no break for either one of us until we see the sun shining through the kitchen window or I scream that I can't take anymore."

Tim survived over six hours of constant pounding sex. The sky had turned to the pre-dawn grey, there were streaks of red and yellow coming through the window but there was no direct sunlight.

Tim had fallen asleep or passed out. He awoke to find that Janice had tied his wrists and hung him from a beam running across the ceiling.

Janice had a smile of pure ecstasy. "You performed well for an older man, Tim. But now I'm going to show what really pushes me over the edge."

Tim screamed when he saw the collection of scalpels and knives. He continued to scream as she was true to her word; every inch of Tim's flesh was peeled away. His screams seemed to bring her more pleasure.

She fed him liquids that stimulated every nerve ending. She rubbed her naked body against him, causing him to convulse. From time to time she would ask "Happy, lover?" or "Enjoying yourself?"

After hours of pain, he passed out. His dreams were filled with screaming, and blood. A tidal wave covered him in its wake—he realized she had thrown a bucket of water in his face. The water ignited a fire over his entire being. He gritted his teeth, but did not scream, until she covered him in salt. She massaged it over his stomach then reached between his legs and squeezed until the salt clung to his body.

By early evening, Janice sat on the table and looked at her handiwork. He was still alive, but useless to her. His mind was gone; there were no functioning nerve endings anywhere on his body. Again she showered. Carrying her clothes, she stood in front of him naked.

Well, Tim, was all this worth dying for?" she asked as she caressed her body. Slowly, she dressed, allowing him to watch. His jaw moved, but there were no lips to smack or tongue to cluck.

"Well lover, it's time to say goodnight. Places to go, people to see. Oh, don't worry. I'm not going to leave you dripping all over the floor." she laughed. "By the way, do you like barbecue?"

She struck the head of a road flare and tossed it into a corner filled with paper and rags, "Be a lamb and scream loud enough for me to hear down the road will you?"

The wood cabin was old, and the dry wood couldn't resist the fire. Flames surrounded him. He heard her laughing as the car backed out of the gravel driveway. She headed back to civilization and new victims.

Tim began to scream, not because the flames had reached him, but because they could not reach him fast enough.

What is Your Name?

Iawoke slowly, groggy, not sure where I was or why. I tried to get up only to discover that my body would not move. Slowly, my eyes opened and began to focus on my surroundings.

"Ah...good evening, sir," The disembodied voice commented. I could not see him nor could I move to discover his location. Looking down, I saw ropes. I was being held against my will—I was a prisoner.

I had no idea who my captors were or why they had me tied to a straight-backed wooden chair. "Who was behind the voice? What did he want with me? Terrified, I decided to say nothing until I could determine just what this voice demanded of me.

"Shall we begin again, sir?" the voice echoed in my head. He slowly walked from behind me and faced me dead on. His tall, thin, cheekbones seemed to jut through his skin. "You have been unconscious for two days, sir. It would appear that you have your days and nights confused," his laugh ripe with knowing sarcasm.

"Let's start with simple questions ... what is your name? Why is the Duke so interested in you?" I stared at him, blankly; He thought I knew the answer. I didn't.

As I remained silent, his smile disappeared. He dragged a chair in front of me, straddled it and stared directly into my eyes. "I am just about through playing nice with you. I have wasted a week; I don't care what the Duke commands about keeping you in one piece, or keeping you alive. If you don't start talking, I am going to take you apart, piece by piece, and enjoy your every scream."

Again, I stared at my inquisitor. I allowed myself a guarded smile ... a challenge to him. His threats meant nothing to me; if he only knew, I was a lost soul. It wasn't that I refused to answer, I couldn't. *I don't know my name.*

"What's your name," he continued. "Where are you from? How old are you? Why does the Duke want you questioned? He finally lost control and struck me in the face. I could smell the blood ... my blood. I licked my lip, the warm coppery taste in my mouth. Once again, I smiled, only this time it was a big toothy grin. "You rush to judgment sir and your rash actions will be your undoing." My first words to my captor with a voice that was raspy, un-recognizable.

His face turned blood red, sweat beaded on his forehead and trickled into his eyes. It stung his eyes. He stood, wiping his face with his sleeve. Saying nothing he walked away frustrated.

Others appeared and released my hands, feet, and chest from the chair, but chains replaced the ropes on my wrists. I was hoisted to my feet, just beyond my tiptoes. My body swung slightly two and fro.

A door opened behind me. The sweet voice of an angel spoke the most interesting words ... "Why is he dressed? Strip him and attach the cables. Time is short. The Duke will be here by dawn and he demands answers."

She wore a short, bright red dress, low cut, revealing all her assets. Under other circumstances, I would have made up things just to keep her near me. I wanted to be home, wherever that was—asleep in my own bed, cuddled up to a beautiful woman who wasn't trying to kill me. She sneered at me. "What do you have to say to me, dog?" Her voice was grating. It challenged me to ignore her question. She walked toward me, her red dress accentuating every curve. I devoured her with my eyes.

I returned her smile and took a hungry survey of her body. "Madam," my voice gruff and dry, "I hope you don't mind my saying that you look good enough to eat. I just don't know where to start."

"Smart Ass ...," she countered. "I will give you a new song to sing."

I was hoisted higher off the floor. Wet straps were attached to my feet.

The guy with the runaway check bones stuffed a wet sponge in my mouth. The water tasted foul, but the liquid soothed my dry throat.

The relief was short lived as the first jolt of electricity coursed through my body, my muscles convulsed, locking my jaws into the sponge. My body vibrated for what seemed an eternity. Just as suddenly as it started, it stopped. The woman applied the electricity to various areas of my body four additional times. She loved her work, that one.

"Now, my friend," she said as she pulled the sponge from my mouth. "A simple question … What is your name!" she screamed.

I heard her, but I couldn't tell her my name, I didn't know it. Instead, I turned my face into her neck and took a deep breath. I licked her and whispered, "You taste magnificent."

She stepped back, anger flashed in her eyes. "Enjoyed yourself, did you?" she asked. "I am anything but cheap. Let's see if you can afford the payment for your little treat."

A large man stepped in front of her and bowed. He displayed a whip with sharp pieces of metal attached to the ends of the strands.

"Thirty save one," I heard her say. The whipping started. She sat in front of me. Her legs spread wide, skirt riding high. One of her hands touched her breast. She stared into my eyes. Each strike of the whip produced a wet sound—flesh being torn from my body. Swinging from the rope, I jerked from the pain, providing my tormentor with new targets. My wrists bled as the rope tightened with each lash.

Her hands began to explore the rest of her body as her eyes devoured my bloody frame. She too jerked as she sat in the chair, but for other reasons. She was lost in some erotic dream.

The whipping continued; at the count of twenty-nine, a shriek of release escaped her throat and a scream of pain from mine as she reached up and grabbed me in my most sensitive area. We finished together, I hung limp and continued to swing. I fought to stay conscious.

The thin man whispered in her ear. She pushed him backwards, angered by his interruption. Slowly she stood, her eyes glued to mine as though searching for my soul. She stepped closer to admire my wounds.

Someone handed her a drink in a long-stemmed glass—she wet her lips, regaining her strength—the mood had ended and it was time to begin the questioning, again.

Her attending goon gave her a wet sponge. She wiped my face and wet my lips. The water this time was cool, sweet, and comforting.

Leaning closer she whispered, "Now that we've shared something special, tell me your name?"

Again, I smelled her neck. This time she stepped into me allowing me another deep breath. Her perfume was now mixed with her arousal. Again, I tasted her neck, only now, I hope I left her my mark. I sucked and nipped her neck just above her shoulder. *Her taste could heal a dying man,* I thought, *and that would be me.*

"Ah, my love," I replied, "should I tell you what I know, our romance will end, and I don't think I can live without you." She backhanded me, full fist, probably breaking my jaw and instantly causing a black and swollen eye.

My smile was lopsided; I was beyond feeling pain. I was enjoying the game, a man with nothing to lose. Had she known that, she might have taken a different path.

She licked the blood from her knuckles and spit it to the floor. Ah, what a waste, I thought. All secrets are in the blood, she didn't know how to find them.

"Open the window," she commanded, "It smells of sweat, bloody meat, and man." She turned her back to me. A leather satchel sat on a table, opening the case; she extracted a variety of implements of doom. "The Duke will be here shortly and he demands answers. Our games of love are over," she murmured to herself, "time to go to work."

I took a deep breath; I would now know true pain. Since I knew nothing, they would never have their answers. I rocked my body, swinging myself around to view out the window.

The ocean was near; I could smell it ... I could all but see it on the horizon. Looking out ... I saw the moon. The sight of it mesmerized me, it gave me energy, and it changed me. It was a full moon and it filled the window frame.

I took a deep breath feeling strength return to my body. The moon did the rest. The raw meat rack that had been my back was changed in an instant. Some inner beast had found a way to escape my broken body.

The chains that held me aloft broke like straw. I dropped silently to the floor as my body continued to change. Now on all fours, I grew in size, strength and shape.

The big man watched me as my body changed. Fixated, he delayed a few seconds, before reaching for his whip. I stood upright as he lashed out. I grabbed the end of the whip, and pulled him to me. Wrapping the strands of leather and metal around his neck and gave it a tug. The metal bit into his neck. He would have screamed, had he been able.

The Thin Man ran for the door but I was now stronger and faster. I leapt forward, my muzzle forcing its way under his chin. I ate his throat, feeding with the frenzy of a person who had been starved for days and placed at a banquet table.

My transformation happened so quickly the lady in red hadn't noticed her devastating change in circumstances.

"My angel," I growled. She turned with a scalpel in her hand. I was already halfway across the room bounding toward her. She lunged, scalpel thrust in front of her. I batted her hand away, and the scalpel flew across the room.

There was banging at the door. Men were shouting the Prince had arrived. They had come to take me to his castle. The locked door was made of multiple layers of thick steel. I knew I had time to settle accounts before additional captors could arrive and open the door.

Once again, she tried to backfist me. I caught her hand and jerked her to me. She screamed as her shoulder dislocated. "My love," I growled softly into her ear, "I have paid your price in full. Now, you must pay your debt … to me."

My claw of a hand drug down the front of her dress. Her clothing fell away; the red streak of blood followed the trail of my claw.

"You got yours … now I want mine." My voice vibrated as I pulled her close, licking the trail of blood down her body. I held her tight with one arm and lowerede her to the floor, staring down, soaking in her beauty.

Her eyes grew wide with fear as I entered her. Curiosity overtook her as she discovered I did not intend to rip out her throat. Moaning, she smiled and arched her hips, she challenged my manhood and I could not help myself but to accept and overpower her.

She was almost my match. I was running short of time, the door was weakening. I stood, she remained in my arms and impaled as we stumbled backwards against the door, our added weight held the hinges and slowed the progress of those outside.

She moaned, screamed and went limp again in my arms. Pain, pleasure or living a nightmare, I really didn't know. I gently lay her on the floor. One last intake of breath, her scent now registered forever in my mind.

"I will return, my angel, when the time of whelping is due." If she could hear, she might understand. The only humanness left of me now were my thoughts of survival.

I climbed through the opened window. Looking back at my angel lying in the floor, the metal door gave way. I knelt on the window ledge ... "Tell the Duke, my half-brother, my name is Larry Talbot ... King of the werewolves!" I jumped.

I howled as I ran up the deserted street. My cry answered from somewhere in the mountains. I headed for the ocean. I would remain among humans and look after my new bride. She and my son must be protected from my brother and his army.

Closet Monster

"**O**kay, boy. I'm through wasting time. Get your butt in bed and get to sleep." The man commanded.

"But Daddy, it's dark and there are monsters." the boy whined, "I don't want to be eaten by the monsters."

"I ain't your daddy, you little brat, but that won't stop me from dragging you up the stairs, beating your ass and throwing you in the bed if I have to. Now move," he commanded.

The boy climbed the stairs, one at a time, tears streaming down his face. He watched his stepfather glare at him with hate filled eyes. "Please, come with me." The boy pleaded softly, seeking mercy.

"Fine, if it will get you out of my hair, I'll put you to bed, but if I hear one word, you will spend tomorrow standing at your desk in school," he growled.

The man removed himself from the recliner. Beer in hand.

The young boy scurried up the steps as the man quickly followed. "I don't know why you have to believe in monsters at the age of eight. You are a wimp and a sissy." The tirade continued as the man climbed the steps and stomped towards the child's room. He was obviously angry and threatened the boy within an inch of his life.

The boy ran into his room, leaped into bed, and dove under the covers.

The man stood in the doorway. He surveyed the room, glaring down at the bed. "Okay, where are all your monsters?" he demanded.

"I am here to do battle with the boy eating monsters so he can get to sleep and I can have a peaceful evening before his mom gets home from work." He said, challenging the mythical creatures. He raised his fists, hoping to scare the kid into submission. It was tiring having to follow the little wimp to bed every night.

The man knew the routine. He looked under the bed, behind the dresser, toy box, desk … all the furniture; then stepped to the closet. "Are your useless monsters in here? Is this why the door is shut? Your monster is hiding among your smelly shoes and shirts!" The man laughed as he threw open the closet door, only to find the boys clothes neatly hung, his games on the shelf and shoes lined neatly along the floor.

The man turned and saw the surprised look on the boy's face. "What?" He screamed. "Did you have some kind of plan? Did you have a trap set that didn't go off? I'll bet all your crap was supposed to fall on my head."

Red faced, filled with anger, the man charged towards the bed, both hands clenched in powerful fists ready to strike the boy as he cringed in his bed. "I'm going to beat you until even your mother won't recognize you." He yelled. A long green tail, covered in scales, and quick as lightening, whipped from under the bed, taking both of the man's feet out from under him. He fell flat on his back, the air knocked from his lungs.

The creature slid out from under the bed. It stood seven feet tall on its hind legs. Its scales glowed with excitement, while yellow eyes shined like an early morning sunrise. The monster looked at the boy, shook its head and growled. He gave the boy a toothy grin and a thumbs up sign.

The boy smiled and laughed, "Hank, meet Asshole; he's the stepdad I've been telling you about. Asshole, meet Hank; he is the monster you were threatening that lives in my closet. Actually, he just visits when I need him. He visits a lot of kids who need help from people like you."

Hank reached down and picked up the man by the neck, turned to the boy and said in a musical voice, "Oh! He will do nicely. Sorry I wasn't waiting in the closet, I was running late from another house. There is a very nice little girl that needed protecting from her uncle."

The creature looked at the man. His smile showed rows of sharp teeth. "Asshole, my family offers you an official invitation to dinner ... Oops; I mean you are invited for dinner."

Hank looked at the young boy. "I'll see you when I see you. Hope your mom makes a better choice next time."

The creature slid under the bed, dragging the screaming stepfather with him. The bed did not bounce as both squeezed through the small open space between the bed and the floor.

The boy looked under the bed and noticed a shrinking, glowing circle fading in the floor.

He laid his head back on his pillow, and smiled. His mom will miss having a man around the house, but the boy knew she would soon find another, she always did. The boy hoped it would be someone nice, for a change, but if not, there is always Hank.

The Caress

She stood, a motionless silhouette in the full length window. Being thirty stories high provided a wonderful view of the city below. She could name each street and park. The same streets she had endlessly searched for what seemed a lifetime.

It was well past midnight and she was alone, waiting. Expecting him to arrive hours ago, she chose the sheer full-length beige dressing gown he had brought her from one of his trips abroad.

The sheer silk material felt like feathers as it hugged her body in all the right places. Her right arm and shoulder were bare, the left covered from shoulder to wrist by the sheer fabric. The slightest light showed her skin beneath the material. Covered, yet bare, she felt delicious and believed that he would rush to her arms when he saw her.

She had spent most of the late afternoon waiting. Now the sky was black, the black that can only be seen when a person is far above the city lights. It was the dark of the moon. She pictured herself as a fairy princess awaiting her prince to rescue her from the depths of a dragon-protected cave.

She stepped onto the window seat and pressed her face against the glass. A tear drifted down her cheek and wet the glass. She realized that her prince had abandoned his prize.

She felt herself dying inside. Without him she would wither, as a garden left untended, the frost of winter would destroy her.

Is this how the woman she replaced felt on the night he brought me into his life? She asked herself. Did his previous lover realize that she was about to be cast aside, no longer needed by the man she had come to love?

Could she return to the hardships of her life before he engulfed her soul? The life she had lived outside these rooms and studio? He made her feel accomplished, confident, and successful. He had taken her to art openings and sold some of her work. Without him, she would return to the life of an unknown painter and a paid courtesan, no longer the exalted queen of his world.

Her arms stretched to the top of the glass, her skin cool against the expansive pane. Could she break through the glass and plunge to the street below? She could not live without him; she could not survive the anguish of not being a part of his life.

She didn't hear him arrive. He simply stepped up behind her and engulfed her with his arms. "You are beautiful," he whispered, and then kissed her neck. His hands slid up her arms to her shoulders. He held her tight. She felt overpowered and submitted willingly to his superior strength.

Slowly, his fingers traveled down the side of her body. His dominance excited her beyond measure. Her body quivered as his hands captured and squeezed the edge of her breasts then slowly and painfully journeyed to her hips. He pulled her lower body to him, molding his body to hers. His fingers explored her, their mission was to tease and tantalize.

She lowered her hands to her sides. He intertwined his fingers with hers. His fingers, skimmed their way higher, teasing her arms, sending electric sparks up her arms.

Her body continued to tremble, vibrating at his closeness. She devoured his touch, strength, and smell. Her craving for him was unquenchable as though he were the only drug that brought her to life.

With increasing strength and hunger, his right arm slid from her neck and cupped her breast, the left followed. The tips of his fingers squeezed and pinched her nipples. The fabric of the gown intensified the feelings as his thumb and forefinger ignited her lust from fire to blast furnace. A deep sigh issued from her parted lips.

His hands warmed the material with their touch; it set her on fire as they ever so slowly slid down her chest and stomach.

They stopped at the center of her hunger and squeezed, pushing her into him. She felt his need and relaxed against him.

"The material feels like skin, I feel goose bumps on your body." He whispered.

She whimpered again as his fingers glided their way to her hips and down the outside of her thigh. He traced the small designs over the material and set her heart racing until she thought it would break through her chest.

He reached around her waist and pulled her tighter. He kissed the back of her neck through her long blonde hair.

She continued to press against him, her need and passion rising with each breath. It had been so long since his last visit. She wanted him to take her into his arms and possess her in ways that only his imagination could complete. She wanted him to fulfill her fantasies, which thrilled and terrified her at the same time.

"You love me, yes?" he asked as his hands reached her chin, pulling her head back to his shoulder. He bit her ear. She shivered with feelings of unknown terror and pleasure.

"Yes." she moaned. Her fingers buried in his thighs. She wanted him to take command, claim her as his own, a spoil of victory.

Again, he pulled her head back, stretching the throat taunt, he licked the side of her neck. His lips lingered at the beating vein, "You are mine to keep, mine to do as I please? You will provide my every desire," his voice commanded softly.

He pushed himself boldly into her, molding her to the glass. His uniform felt coarse against her skin, and the thin fabric. Their bodies became one.

He was proposing to her, she would be his wife. "Oh yes." Her answer so soft he knew what she said only by the vibrations in her throat.

She leaned deeper into him as her fingers dug deeper into his thighs, her legs unable to hold her weight. She did not want to appear weak. She wanted to be strong, to return to him all that he was about to give to her. She would be his equal.

His left arm caressed her neck and turned her face to his. It allowed him to lift her onto her toes and kiss her lips as his right hand slid into a small pocket hidden under his epaulet. He turned placing a knee in the small of her back; he grabbed her long hair at the scalp and yanked back. A quiet scream escaped from her throat as his right hand embedded the scalpel deep into her neck.

So sharp, she didn't feel the blade penetrate her body, just behind the ear. She felt a burn; thought it was her uncontrolled lust for him. She drove her tongue into his mouth, her own passion now forced to escape or cause her to explode. His teeth captured the invading organ and bit it off.

He chewed the meat and smiled as the blade continued its journey. Screaming, she sprayed blood on the window. She tried to pulled away, shocked by his violence. The blade finished it travels to her other ear.

Her neck opened like a gaping mouth, blood blasted onto the window; her struggling body became a brush against the glass creating a death mural for the world to admire. Her body went limp, sliding to the foot of the window. He arranged her body as it lay on the seat below the window.

Her struggles would be described as her greatest piece of modern art. He was anxious to examine the finer qualities of her painting with the rising sun.

He left her body where it lay, walked over to the bar and poured himself a drink. *Now, a nice shower,* he thought. As pre-arranged, all evidence of his life-drained palette was removed by the time he returned to the room; his minions eliminated all evidence of the violence. Her masterpiece, however, remained for his enjoyment.

Tomorrow, he would replace the glass and add her 'Masterpiece in Red' to his gallery. When word was released that she had left the world of art, someone would buy her last creation for a great deal of money.

Collectors, he thought, *always have more money than brains.* In a month, perhaps two he would find another. A new brush would enter the studio. He would groom her until she was ready to create her final masterpiece.

Double Dare

"I double dare you ... I double dog dare you!" she said, her voice belittling and full of sarcasm,

"Let me tell you, Cherry. There was no way I could turn down the challenge of a double dog dare. Of course, I should have known that there was a hidden agenda behind her words, but I couldn't let a girl, a cheerleader, get the better of me.

The old Stevenson Mansion sat on the outskirts of town. It was the oldest home in village, but no one had lived there for over forty years. There were stories that old Silas Stevenson had killed over sixty children on the estate between 1875 and 1910. It was also rumored that several of his descendants enjoyed his sick taste for killing and so did their wives. They were known to be a cruel family that had run the county for generations.

People said his ghost and the ghosts of other family members who had died violently, haunted the property. They relived their gory deeds, debasing the spirits of those they had already killed. Some said they even killed trespassers and tortured those spirits along with the rest.

Buyers and renters of the old property never stayed long in the house. They would leave in the middle of the night without any explanation. None of us believed in ghosts, yet, even high school seniors never went on the property to party, make out, or explore the buildings.

"Before I agree, I want to know the reward. If this is a double-dog dare, the reward must be something I really want." My hope was that this would make her take back the double dare. Breaking into the mansion terrified me. If the reward was small, no way it was worth it.

It didn't work, and again she stared at me with a half grin. "Hmmmm," she said, "those overcoming great challenges receive great rewards." She smiled sweetly. She knew she had just the right hook to suck me in and get me into the mansion.

"If you go to the mansion and bring me something of value from the master bedroom, your reward is me. If you fail, you get nothing." Not only did she give me a challenge, but also, she left me no choice but to comply.

I stared at her in disbelief as she continued. "First, I will allow you to photograph me for a full hour, anyway you wish, dressed, naked, whatever. If you just want to stare, my perfect body and face will be yours. This is a look but don't touch basis." She turned in a circle, hiking her short cheerleader skirt. She was a tease, and knew how to get my attention.

"Second, I will allow you to take me to the Spring Dance." She gave me a slow, deep hug. Her body rubbed against mine as she hummed some unknown tune and swayed to her own music.

"Now that I have your attention," she laughed. "If I believe the treasure is truly valuable, you may receive a third reward. I will allow you to take me to bed for a solid two hours after the dance."

"You can't be serious, Iris," I exclaimed, "You're the captain of the cheerleading team, the most popular girl at school and I am a book worm. Besides, you date Jim Thornton, the quarterback; he would never allow me to take you to the dance. Why would you double-dare me with this reward, knowing Jim will break every bone in my body? He would beat me up just for looking at you, let alone taking you to the dance. Plus, I'm not worthy to date someone in your social group. I would be more than a step down for you when people see us together."

"Easy," she smirked, "All the jocks think they have the world by the tail and the cheerleaders are a treat they can use at their command. Jim refused the dare, and as a matter of fact, so did the rest of the team. I told him and the team if I found someone who was brave enough to take the dare that I was going to go to the dance with him. I also told Jim that if he harmed a hair on the head of this brave sole I would rip his balls off. If you complete the dare, it will put them in their place. So Todd, are you man enough to take the double-dog dare now that you know the challenge and that I am the reward?"

I was dumbfounded and shocked by what had been proposed. I stared at her blond hair and fantastic body. She was unashamed about her looks. A most worthy reward. She even posed a few times, showing just enough skin to ignite a sixteen year old boy into a lusting animal. She had me. I took the dare.

"I'll go right now," I said, excited with the prospect of fulfilling many fantasies.

"Slow down Speed Racer," she said, grinning with her perfect teeth. "You will arrive at the property at ten o'clock tonight. The gate will be unlocked and open. Drive to the front door. Find your way into the house. You have two hours to go through the house, find the master bedroom and an object of value. I will be waiting at the end of the drive. Don't be late; I won't extend the deadline past midnight."

I asked her about the object of value, but all she would tell me is that I would know the item when I found it. If I were wrong, there would be no reward.

I agreed and added to the terms that the photo session would take place on Saturday and the third reward would take place on a night of my choice, not on the night of the dance. I explained that I wanted to be able to claim her three times and not bundle everything into one meeting.

Iris nodded her head in agreement. "Who knows, if you work out, this could be more than a three shot event." Smiling, she turned and walked away.

I turned onto the estate at nine-fifty-five and slowly made my way up the meandering drive. Arriving at the covered entry area, I parked the car and gathered my equipment. I knew I had a two-hour window to accomplish my task. *Why did everything need to be finished by midnight and not dawn?*

There were no lights; the full moon lit the grounds but darkened the shadows beneath the overhang. The place was a mess, overgrown weeds, broken bricks, all the grit and wild growth that comes from years of abandonment.

The front door was solid oak, and locked. None of the past owners had bothered to change the locks and I had a selection of keys that I hoped would open the door. Unfortunately, none of them worked. I walked around to the back of the house, looking for a way in.

Windows were beyond my reach; basement windows were locked and too small for me to gain entrance, but I did find a sunroom with French doors. The doors were locked, but I used my pocketknife to jimmy the door lock until the door creaked open. I had used twenty minutes of my allotted time.

I made my way around covered furniture, fallen fixtures, dirt, grime, and the make shift dens of various animals living in the house. My imagination ran wild as I examined the years of accumulated trash. My mind kept telling me there were creatures in this house and they wanted my soul. I should have run, I needed to run, but I continued my quest because the thought of not winning my bet with Iris drove me on.

From time to time, I heard sounds. I convinced myself they were coming from animals living in the long abandoned nooks and crannies of the old house. *Maybe it is temperature changes causing the house to groan.* I thought. A couple of times I thought I heard a muffled scream and crying, but I knew there was no one in the house but me.

After checking the ground floor, I cautiously made my way up the stairs. I stayed close to the wall. A few stair boards cracked as I climbed the once grand staircase. I was thankful that the boards did not break and send me flying.

It was ten-forty-five. I was on the second floor and I had not found the master bedroom. As I explored the third floor, I thought I heard the sounds of laughter. Was I going to be the butt of a practical joke? Was all of this just an elaborate ruse to make me the laughing stock of the whole school? Were the cheerleaders and jocks sitting outside the front gate laughing?

I searched the top floor. At eleven-ten, I discovered the master bedroom. Another moan echoed through the hall as I opened the door. The room was huge, and took up half of the third floor. The bedroom was bigger than my whole house. Something odd, this room appeared cleaner than the rest of the house. There were no animal tracks on the floor. It seemed nothing living wanted to enter this room. It was unsettling. The room was cold, but despite the chill, I was sweating. I felt sick to my stomach and had to force myself to keep searching the room.

I felt set up by Iris and her friends, but the promise of the fantasy drove me on. There wasn't much furniture in the room. I checked the walls and floors for hidden places or secret passages.

That's when I found a loose board along the edge of the wall. I pried it open and found a small china doll wrapped in linen. It was old and delicate. This would be my prize. Relieved to be done with this house for good, I tucked the doll under my shirt and walked into the hallway. I only had a few minutes left to get out of the house and off the grounds.

The house grew colder. It was ten degrees cooler in the hallway. Someone or something was watching me.

As I flew down the stairs, taking two steps at a time, I felt something brush past me. A cold wind seemed to pass through me. Scared, I could feel a presence. It was growing, getting stronger. I could feel it lurking in the shadows, watching, waiting. Terrified and nearly paralyzed with fear I forced myself to push toward the front door.

I was running out of time. A clock chimed the first stroke of midnight. Joke or not, I didn't dare be late. I had to get out, to get off this property. *What if they close the gate? What if I'm locked in? God help me.*

I broke into a cold sweat as I remembered the stories of Old Man Stevenson hunting trespassers.

If this is a joke, I just might gain some respect from the jocks by completing the dare. With a little luck, I'll get out of this place alive, and be able to walk the halls at school with a big smile on my face. There were many *ifs* and I did not have time to stop and think about them.

Leaving the nightmare house behind me, I jumped in my car. Thank God it started. I raced down the driveway, headlights turned off. I didn't want a wandering police car to see the lights and investigate. I pulled through the gate at the last chime of midnight. No Iris. I got out of my car and called her name, just in case.

"What did you find, Todd?" she asked. She stepped onto the driveway. She seemed to appear out of nowhere just inside the gate. "Not to worry, someone has to lock up the place. If you had run late, we would have been stuck inside, together. Who knows, you might have enjoyed the experience." She laughed.

Personally, I didn't think it was very funny, but I was outside the gate and had the treasure.

Iris walked to the gate. "Well, what treasure did you bring me, Todd?"

I reached under my shirt and pulled out the china doll. It was about eight inches tall. The clothing was discolored and disintegrating. She held the doll in both hands.

Her eyes examined the object; her touch was delicate as she traced its shape. "You've done well, Todd, very well. I haven't seen this treasure in years."

She reached out, pulling me to her; pulling me back inside the property. She hugged me; her tight grip took my breath away. She was cold, ice cold, and it felt like she was claiming the heat from my body. Why hadn't I noticed that before?

She stepped beyond the edge of the driveway onto the sidewalk. Holding the doll towards the house, she yelled. "The Talisman has been found, *Old Man*. I am free! I curse you and send you to hell."

A yellow red flame shot through the house. A man's scream pierced the night. The house sat silent, a thin veil of mist hung at the windows. I thought I saw faces in the mist ... but that couldn't be, could it?

"Thank you, Todd." Iris whispered as she kissed my cheek. "You have done well. I now give you your true reward."

She pointed the doll towards the house. "My sisters and brothers, this boy has set me free. The *Old Man* is banished, but another will take his place.

Continue the fight until everyone is free."

Her eyes turned black. "Sorry Todd, but your lust is your undoing. I was one of the spirits trapped in the house. Each decade, one of us is set free. We must seek revenge against the ruling spirit of the house. Failure means returning to this hell house, to wait for another chance at freedom.

"The *Old Man* is my grandfather. Now he resides in hell, thanks to you. Another ghostly family member will take his place. Once all the family members have been dispatched to hell, the spirits dwelling here will be set free.

It's not all bad. You will enjoy some of the spirits; there are girls and boys, and you can do with them what you wish. They too have ways to make you feel their pain. And the leader will spend time with you, and will strive to give you pain, a great deal of pain. She kissed me, softly, passionately then pushed me back into the driveway, closed the gate leaving me locked inside.

"Oh, had you failed to leave the grounds, you would have been locked on the property and Grandfather would have hunted you down. Had you failed to find the talisman, but gotten off the grounds in time, I would have remained the plaything of my tormentors.

I am truly sorry Todd. It seems unfitting to reward your bravery with entrapment." She faced the house and commanded, "As a newly freed spirit, and as the destroyer of the *Old Man,* I grant one spirit the opportunity to find freedom every five years instead of ten."

She chose her words carefully, giving me direction and guidance. "When you return to the house, you must choose an object in your possession. The new leader will hide the object. For each champion there is a talisman. When found, the spirit will be set free and the living being will take their place.

If the spirit fails in its mission to recover the talisman, she or he must return to the house and wait his or her turn for another attempt at freedom.

I heard the voices of the trapped spirits call to me. Screams and laughter echoed in my brain. I attempted to climb the gate to escape, but was repelled by an invisible force.

A mist floated from the house, it seemed to recognize me as it drifted toward me. I felt myself begin to fade. Joining the mist, I joined the embodied spirits of the house.

"Three hundred years have passed. I have grown weary waiting for my chance at freedom. You have brought me that freedom my sweet Cherry. You recovered my item." I tossed the ring of old keys, "I am free only because you handed it to me before midnight. Tragically, you have failed to make it off the property in time. Now, the house claims your soul. You are now their plaything and they play rough."

"Don't worry; there are many activities and much to do in the house. I hope you enjoy screaming. Screaming happens a lot in that house.

Because you failed to leave the property on time, you will never be allowed to rejoin the world of the living, however there is always the possibility that you will one day become one of the adults and escape the mansion by entering hell, in a thousand years or so."

Did You See That?

"**D**id you see that?" Nick exclaimed. He and Tony sat at the bar drinking beer as they 'people watched' using the reflection in the wall length mirror.

"See what?" Tony asked. "There's been nothing going on in this place for the past hour. I'm thinking we should go someplace with a television or at least some music."

Nick turned to his friend. "Man, how could you have missed it? It must have been a ghost or something. It just floated all the way across the bar. Look, there goes another one!" Nick pointed to the mirror. "I think this place is haunted."

Tony looked at his friend. "You are unbelievable. Tomorrow is Halloween; this place is known as *The Graveyard*. They probably have some sort of projector running your ghosts across the mirror. I'm surprised the locals aren't bringing their kids around to look through the windows at the spooks."

Nick turned again and stared out the window. "Speaking of locals, nobody is out there. This whole neighborhood is dead. Plus, it's dark, I wonder what time it is?" he asked himself. "It seems odd, it's dark, people are off work, and yet no one is stopping by for a drink."

As if on cue, the front door opened, and a young couple walked in. They talked quietly and took a seat at the bar. They held hands, facing one another, staring into each other's eyes.

The bartender walked up to them, "Jodi, Harold what can I get you?" he asked as he stared down the young woman's top.

"Same as always, Jack, two hot spiced wines and the booth in the back," the man answered. He smiled at Jack, "and keep 'em coming." He patted the woman's backside as they turned and headed towards a booth.

People slowly arrived at the Graveyard. Several sat at the bar and watched the mirror. From time to time, someone would point and smile as a ghostly presence floated along its surface. Nick noticed that each time someone made a comment about one of the ghosts, they would move to a table or booth. A few short minutes later, a person would walk out of the back room and join them at their booth or table. The weird thing was that the person who joined them looked like the ghost in the mirror.

"Something strange is going on here, Tony. I think the patrons are picking out ghosts to keep them company." Nick said. He watched as a ghost with flowing long hair glided across the mirror. She looked at Nick and smiled. "Tony, I think she wants me," he said pointing at the image. Tony looked up.

"There's nothing there, you idiot. You are obsessed with ghosts tonight. It's time to get out of here."

The two were just getting off their stools when a tall young blonde woman entered from the back. She walked hand-in-hand with a shorter woman with raven hair. Both were dressed in deep red short skirts and low cut blouses. They smiled at Tony and Nick and seemed to float to where they were standing.

"You can't be leaving all ready," the blonde said to Nick. "We just got here, and it's barely ten. The night is young, many adventures lie ahead." Her accent sounded European. Nick thought she might be from Ireland or Scotland.

The raven-haired beauty stared at Tony. Her emerald eyes seemed to look deep into his soul. Licking her lips, she whispered, "Morana chose me for you. I am lucky; you are a hero among men while your friend is weak. I can see that your needs are strong. I hope my skills will bring us together as one."

The blonde looked at the two men. "I'm so sorry for being rude. I am Morana and my friend is named Alexei." Morana stroked Nick's cheek. "Would you care to buy two ladies a drink and talk for a while? We must leave soon, and it seems a shame to not spend the time with two handsome men."

The bartender approached the foursome; Alexei smiled and ordered four hot-spiced wines. She asked the bartender to bring the drinks to the last vacant booth. He nodded and prepared their drinks.

Tony followed his friend and the two women. He noticed that the young couple in the back booth had company. A second woman had joined them. They were going at it pretty hot and heavy. There were several empty glasses on the table and the three were lost in their own world of twisting flesh and soft moans.

Nick noticed too and smiled. He was thinking, *This is some bar. Anything goes in here.*

Every table had ordered the hot-spiced wine. He decided that the drink choice had something to do with the way people were acting. Ghosts or no ghosts, Nick decided he was going to have a good time.

The men ended up in the middle of the round booth. The bartender brought the drinks. "You're new here, so I brought two rounds. After the first taste, you will probably down the drink. The second is for sipping," he said smiling.

The bartended was right. The first glass went down quickly. It didn't take long for the second glass to follow the first. The girls, however, sipped the wine. As if on cue, the bartender delivered four additional glasses. Nick offered to share a glass with Morana, but she smiled and refused. The drink was mesmerizing. Sipping was out of the question. As he drank, his physical desire for the woman grew. He suspected there was something in the wine, but he couldn't stop himself. He kept drinking.

Nick cuddled next to Morana, sliding his hand to her knee. She smiled and nestled closer. Her hand rested on his thigh. "You are a strong and virile young man," she whispered as she nibbled on his ear lobe and slid her hand higher.

Alexei stared into Tony's eyes. "You don't know what to think of me, do you?" she asked. Her eyes had captured his mind and thoughts. He was losing control of himself, but was helpless to stop. He put down his glass, and decided to enjoy her company. I asked Morana to join your friend. We were the last reflections—you were the last customers."

Alexei held his hand as she explained. "There are times when two different worlds align. When it occurs, we can cross over for a while, time seems to stand still and the gods don't care what we do." She kissed him lightly on the lips.

Tony didn't understand but he knew he cared for her. He pulled her closer and hugged her tight. She rested her head on his shoulder; he was lost in her long black hair and vanilla scent. For the first time, he felt content and he was at peace with a woman. Tony had never believed in love at first sight, until now.

Just as Tony was feeling the impact of Alexi, Nick was not shy about his growing desires for Morana. She pushed him for more, daring him to live out his hungers. He was rough as he physically abused her with hands and teeth.

Nick continued to chug the spiced wine. The glasses seemed to refill themselves. Each glass released more of his aggression brought on by years of frustration and failure. He was filled with anger, desire, and lust.

No longer trying to control himself, Nick picked Morana up by the waist and slammed her back down on the table. He impaled himself into her. He growled as he continued to pound her without control. Morana leaned back, screamed in pleasure, and threw herself forward, biting Nick on the shoulder until faint traces of blood seeped through his shirt.

Tony looked at the couple. He tried to separate Nick from the girl, but Nick pushed him away. Mine ... all mine!" he yelled in triumph.

"She has taken him, they are as one. She has taken his soul," Alexei said. "Your actions remain gentlemanly. You are pure of heart and I cannot destroy you. It is time for you to depart this place before it is too late."

Tony stared at the girl. "Let's go together; it looks like the whole bar has gone crazy," he said as he looked at the other tables. People were in all stages of undress, committing acts so vile that Tony's mind could not take it all in.

"Quickly, you must go!" Alexei commanded. She stood and drug Tony towards the door. "Don't look back, just get away!" she cried.

"Come with me," Tony demanded. "This is no place for you." Instead, Alexei pushed him out the door as the first chime of midnight rang in the bar.

Tony saw her turn and run towards Nick and Morana, tearing at her clothing. He screamed for her, tried to open the door. It wouldn't open. Tony heard the clock chime, at the count of six; the bar appeared to glow; first yellow, then red. At ten, the interior of the bar burst into flames. He saw Nick scream in pain as the two beautiful women morphed into hideous creatures. They began to devour him. Those who had joined the patrons at their tables morphed into horrible creatures and devoured their partners.

Tony stared in disbelief. There was no heat coming through the glass, no smoke, other than what rose from inside the bar. He saw Alexei look at him and for an instant; he saw sorrow in her eyes. The transformation of Alexei was total. Mouth open, her gaping fangs glowed in the flames as she took another bite from Nick's chest.

Tony heard the twelfth chime. Midnight, it was a new day. Tony found himself looking through the window of an antique store. "She pushed me out of the bar. She saved me because I am pure of heart," he said aloud. Tony remembered her words, *When our worlds align* ... He was in love with stranger—something from another time and place. He whispered as he began the walk home, "Times change, people change. Perhaps

next year I will join you, my love. Happy Halloween,
Alexei."

Some Day Dreamer ...

The true nightmare of a madman

While the teacher droned on-and-on about the economic strain of the American Civil War, he stared out the window watching the winged dragons fly in circles over the schoolyard. They were small, only two or three feet long, but strong, their muscles rippling as they flew.

One of the dragons would launch itself from the rooftop and plunge down then level off inches above the ground. The playground was their personal obstacle course. The red and green creatures weaved through the swings, slides, and other equipment designed for the smaller children in grade school.

From out of nowhere, she appeared. One second the swing was empty, the next, she was swinging back and forth, as the three dragons began circling her. She was talking to them; they landed beside her, the smallest hanging over her shoulder and the others settled at her feet. They watched her intently as babies listening to their mother. The boy tensed, wondering if the reptiles would eat or cook her with their breath; to his amazement, they seemed to fall asleep.

He couldn't hear what she said or sang, but the girl and the three creatures were close friends. "Freddy Thompson, are you listening to me?" the irritated voice of the teacher invaded his mind. He looked at his teacher, then back out the window. The girl and the dragons were gone.

"I'm sorry Mrs. Everson, something caught my eye and I didn't hear the question." He replied innocently.

"Yeah, something caught your eye, for the last five minutes, young man." her tone was abrasive. "I asked you to recite the Gettysburg Address. If you can complete the speech perfectly, you can remain in class and not go to the principal's office."

Freddy stood at his desk. He knew the words because he actually enjoyed reading about the civil war; the battles and their aftermath were his favorite. He decided to put feeling into his presentation, just as the actor on the History Channel had done last night.

Freddy began his speech, tears formed in his eyes as he imagined himself as President Lincoln. He spoke of the battle and the loss of life and how the United States must again be one country before it destroyed itself. When he finished, there was silence in the room.

"Can you tell me Mr. Thompson, what the words you just recited *mean* ... in your own words?" Again, Freddy spoke with passion about the War, and the great loss of life on both sides, as well as the destruction of cities and farmland in both the North and the South. He explained that this was Lincoln's plea to find a peaceful solution and end the war.

"Well done, Mr. Thompson. Not only will I allow you to stay in class, but you may also go outside during lunch. BUT, no more distractions, I want your full attention the rest of the day." Freddy nodded and quietly sat back down. When the teacher's back was turned he glanced out the window to see if the girl and the dragons had returned, but there was nothing but an empty swing in the schoolyard.

At last, lunch period arrived. Freddy hurried into the schoolyard. He ignored his friends, the soft ball game, and all other activities around him. He searched for the girl. He knew he was something of a daydreamer, but he had never seen things that weren't really there before.

He looked at the top of the building, searching for any movement or something flying high above the playground. The dragons and the girl were gone. He was frustrated. Surely, they felt him watching them and knew he meant them no harm.

At recess, Freddy walked along the edge of the school grounds, searching the bushes and the treetops hoping to find the girl hiding.

The bell announced the end of recess. He would try to keep an eye out for the girl and hope the teacher didn't catch him. His hopes were not high. She had vanished as quickly as she had arrived. For all he knew, she was simply his daydream girl.

As the last three hours of school dragged on, he became anxious as he thought of the girl and wondered if he would ever see her again. Lost in another daydream, Freddy all but jumped out of his seat when the dismissal bell rang. He gathered his things and headed for the door.

The teacher watched him as though she expected him to jump out the window. As he flew out the door, she wondered why he was in such a hurry. She shrugged and gathered her things. It was Friday, and her life extended far beyond the classroom.

Freddy walked slowly around the schoolyard. His eyes searched every shadow and space for the girl. She was nowhere to be found. After hours of searching, he began the slow walk home, alone.

Saturday afternoon, Freddy sat in his room reading. A morning trip to the library had introduced him to the world of Ann McCaffrey. As he read, he realized that the creatures he had seen were fire lizards, not dragons.

He was thinking of the flight the creatures had taken over the school playground; at that moment, one flashed past his window. Staring out his window, he saw her. This time she was standing under the oak tree in the back yard looking up at his window. She wore the same yellow sundress and sandals.

Freddy turned and ran from his room, bounded down the stairs and out the back door. He dove off the porch and sprinted across the back yard only to discover she had vanished.

Dejected, he sat under the tree the rest of the day, waiting ... hoping for her return. There were times, when he thought he saw the creatures from the corner of his eye, but they never came close to him or in full view. He never saw the girl.

That night, he dreamed of her. His imagination filled in the blanks—her eye color, her smile, and the sound of her voice. In his dream, she was perfect. She could be his girlfriend.

He spent Sunday looking out his window, searching. Later he returned to his books. Thanks to McCaffrey's books, he was learning a lot about fire lizards.

Time passed as time does and the school year was coming to a close. He never gave up on his search but saw nothing of the lizards or of the girl. He never found her. Freddy decided his teacher was right; he was a hopeless daydreamer, caught up in his own imaginings.

No matter how much he tried to forget, she never left his mind. The thought of her made him feel good. She felt like home, as if he belonged with her.

Classes ended the first week of June and Freddy was ready for summer. He had lined up several lawn jobs and planned to spend his free time with his friends at the river. His mind and body active, the girl became a quiet memory.

July arrived like a blast furnace. Freddy did his lawn jobs, then went home exhausted, to crash and then recover with several popsicles and sodas. The fourth of July ended with cookouts and fireworks. Best of all, the heat wave broke.

Freddy was sitting on the porch swing enjoying his new action comic when a moving van pulled up across the street. A new station wagon pulled into the driveway and a father, mother, and daughter climbed out of the car. The movers started taking furniture and boxes into the house.

Freddy had no interest in watching new neighbors unload their boxes and returned to his book. He heard a laugh and looked up. From the distance, he could have sworn it was the girl with the fire lizards, but that wasn't possible, she wasn't real.

As more laughter cascaded across the lawn and into the street, he was drawn from the porch swing. Freddie found himself walking across the street, eager to meet his new neighbors. He laughed at himself as he searched the sky, but there were no creatures flying around the house. *You are still lost in that daydream, you romantic.* He thought to himself.

The girl stood behind the family car. She wore a yellow flowered dress and sandals— in her hand was a stuffed golden dragon. Freddy stood at the end of the driveway and stared. Her eyes were blue. When she said "Hello," it was the voice he had heard in his dream.

"Hi yourself," he stuttered. "Welcome to the neighborhood. I'm Freddy."

"I'm Victoria...Vicky. This seems like a nice town, I saw a Pizza Hut on the way to the house," she said lowering her eyes and twisting her foot like some girls do when they are shy.

"I like your fire lizard. Why is he gold?" Freddy continued trying to make conversation.

"Ah, you recognized her. Most people call her a dragon, but she isn't. In Ann's books, you can't ride a lizard." She laughed. She held out her most proud possession. "Being gold makes her the queen," she exclaimed.

"What about the others?" he blurted. "The blue, green, and red, what happened to them?"

The girl took a closer look at the boy. He was a year or two older than her thirteen years. "Oh, they are packed away for now. How did you know I have lizards of different colors?"

"I have seen them all before ... and you too. It was in the spring in the school yard and then again in my back yard." He blurted. "I day dreamed about you in school. You were in my dreams at night. I didn't think you were real, but I couldn't get you out of my mind."

Victoria cocked her head and smiled. "Yes, I saw you before we decided to move here. You were watching me from windows. I wondered if my flying friends were trying to tell me something about my future. I think we are destined to be good friends. Come, meet my parents."

As they turned to walk up the driveway, Vickie gave Freddy the most innocent child-like kiss on his cheek and took his hand. Freddy could have sworn the head of the golden lizard turned, looked at him and smiled. His heart soared. Freddy didn't have much luck with girls, but Vicky was special and her fire lizard approved.

Who knows, he thought. *I think I'll get a bronze lizard of my own. They are the strongest and they mate for a lifetime.*

As they started up the sidewalk, Vickie snuggled closer to him. Freddy smiled as he thought *Vicky will always be my girlfriend. I'm a Some Day Dreamer and I have found the day dream of a lifetime.*

About the Author

Born in East St. Louis, John spent a major portion of his youth in Illinois. He began reading at an early age and soon discovered a love for science fiction and horror. He devoured book after book about vampires, shifters, and dragons.

John holds a degree in journalism from the University of Memphis. His military career included twelve years in Public Affairs. It was there that he honed his writing skills and won multiple awards.

After retiring from the Air Force, he bought a Harley and volunteered with politically active motorcycle organizations. He wrote stories promoting motorcycling, which were published throughout the state of California.

John currently lives in Highland, Illinois with his mother and Bassett hound named Barkley P. Howl.

John invites your comments and thoughts about the book. You can email John at Writerphotographer1946@gmail.com.

To find out where John is appearing visit his website at www.JohnWSmithAuthor.com.